MATANZAS

Cab Dunaway rode south from Raton into a part of New Mexico he had never seen before. A fierce wind drove him like a tumbleweed until three Mexican cowboys stopped him and one aimed a gun at his face.

From that moment until he sat beneath some trees with a beautiful woman almost a month later, Cab Dunaway lived through ordeals few other men could have survived. In fact, other men did not survive those ordeals.

Murder by renegades, cattle-rustling on a scale Cab had never encountered before, and the helpless people these things happened to turned Cab Dunaway into something he had never been before – an avenger who used everything he could think of, even a big herd of cattle, to break the grip of the renegades.

By the same author

Gila Bend
Sixguns and Sam Logan
Apache Wells
Ute Peak Country

MATANZAS

CLINT CUSTER

A Black Horse Western

ROBERT HALE · LONDON

First published in Great Britain 1986

ISBN 0 7090 2346 4

Robert Hale Limited
Clerkenwell House
Clerkenwell Green
London EC1R 0HT

Photoset in North Wales by
Derek Doyle & Associates, Mold, Clwyd.
Printed in Great Britain by
WBC Print Ltd, Bristol.
Bound by WBC Bookbinders Ltd.

One:
Springtime

There were ragged clouds crossing a gunmetal sky trailed by a high wind that cut through clothing like a knife, and out across the open country the dead stalks of last summer's grass fluttered like thin bones, unable to free themselves from the crusted topsoil.

The northern New Mexico world looked more like a bleak winter's heartland than springtime, nor was there a change in sight as the muscular bay horse under Cabot Dunaway humped under the saddle, kept his rump to the biting wind which splayed his black tail, and walked along with his head down, the reins loose, his eyes half closed against stinging bits of sand and soil, his expression one of stolid endurance.

The roominghouse proprietor up at Durham had said a course due south would cut twenty miles off the route followed by the stage road, and while he was probably correct, there were places for shelter along the roadway and out across this god-forsaken prairie country there was not even a decent windbreak.

Dunaway and his bay horse had tried a few deep arroyos, but because for some perverse reason they were invariably open from the north, the bitter wind whistled down through them too, and because it was compressed between earthen walls in the arroyos, it blew harder and seemed colder.

Ordinarily, a rangeman could find some kind of shelter. Up in Colorado, for example, there would have been stone barrancas a man and his horse could shelter behind. And wood to make a fire with.

Down here there were just endless miles of dead grass, grit in the air, and nothing to obstruct the force of the wind. Saving twenty miles under these circumstances was about like cutting off a dog's tail an inch at a time, rather than all at once.

There were not even any cattle. The entire vast panorama was empty of life and movement. If Dunaway had had some idea where he was, perhaps that might have helped, but all he knew for a fact was that there was a town up ahead somewhere called Matanzas – and that was bad enough because a *matanza* was a slaughter ground.

Cab Dunaway knew that much Spanish and not very much more. He had grown up in Missouri, had ridden for cow outfits from Montana to Idaho, then back over through Wyoming and Colorado. During the course of those years he had learned some Spanish. First, inevitably, he had learned the bad words and sentences; the ones a man might use around a cow camp, but not any other place. And finally, he had learned a few other words, but when strung together, they might be understandable, but they were never in a proper context. Mexican cowboys were not common in Montana and Idaho. There were a few in Wyoming and a few more down in Colorado. Spanish was not a language people used in those places, unless they were the rare few *vaqueros*.

But New Mexico was different. He knew that without ever having been any farther south than Raton. Down here Spanish was spoken interchangeably with English, and quite often to the convulsive mirth of the natives, it was spoken as Mexlish, or as Englishcan, or Spanlish. Whatever the jokesters called it, it was basically Border Spanish.

Dunaway was not worried. He'd never had trouble either picking up dialects, or making himself understood, and as he rode with his collar up, head pulled down inside it, and his eyes puckered nearly closed, he didn't care what people spoke, he simply wanted to find a place of shelter – with people or without them, whether he understood them or they understood him.

The bay horse was equally anxious to find shelter. While he could not make a noise to indicate this feeling, there were other ways he could convey his meaning, like having his back humped beneath the saddle and resisting any rein-pressure which might make him turn his head into the scouring wind.

It was the kind of day when a man expected sleet, like daggers of ice. There might have been sleet but for that bitter wind; it kept the roiled atmosphere constantly in a moving turmoil.

Visibility was fair, in spite of the stinging filaments of sand. Dunaway watched continually for a sanctuary. By mid-afternoon he did not care whether it had firewood or not; just a place to protect him from the wind.

It was the powerfully muscled-up bay horse who, without changing pace, raised his head slightly, an indication that something had caught his interest. But in this moonscape of utter desolation that could have been nothing more rewarding than a big rock.

Dunaway saw it, finally, when one of those unpredictable shifts in the wind arrived, sweeping the grit into his face and away from the country on ahead.

There was a subtle but noticeable change in the land-form. Flatness yielded to gentle land-swells, and to the west there were trees. The first Cab Dunaway had seen since the day before. Gradually, as he approached the first low and soft rise of land, he saw more trees, and finally, progressing down the far side of the first landswell he saw what had been holding the attention of his horse.

Three horsemen spread out so that there was about thirty feet between them, blocking his onward progress. They had bandanas over their lower faces, like the Wells Fargo illustrations of road agents. They had carbines jutting upwards beside saddle swells, and they were Mexicans.

Clearly, they had seen him approaching. May have been watching his progress for a long time, for all he knew. One thing he *did* know, they were not going to be friendly. The evidence of this was in the way they sat their horses. It was also evident in the way they allowed him to come within a quarter of a mile, then without haste, drew their handguns.

He did not deviate from his course, but rode up to within a couple of yards of them, and stopped, leaned with both gloved hands atop the saddlehorn and looked steadily at them. There was little to see of their faces, but the huge horns, metal stirrups, the slick forks and loop-through stirrup-leathers were pure Mexican, as were the Chihuahua spurs with rowels nearly as large as small saucers. Their attire too, while not pure Mex *vaquero*, was close enough. In attire they were hybrid Mex *vaqueros* and Southwestern cowboys.

Dunaway let the wind carry his greeting. "*Buenas dias, amigos.*"

The reply came from the stocky, short man in the middle. He raised his sixgun and aimed it; held it like that for almost a full minute. Then he spoke in English with a chili-pepper accent guttural enough to cut with a knife. "Get down from the horse."

Dunaway, having brazened out the menacing pistol, did not obey. If it had been the stocky man's intention to shoot him, he would have done it. Also in English he said, "What do you want?"

"Get down!" commanded the *pistolero*.

Dunaway looked straight down the gunbarrel to the masked face behind it. "Shoot," he said, and moved his right hand off the saddlehorn.

The *vaquero* to the right of the man with the gun

turned and looked at his companion. Then he laughed behind the bandana and Dunaway saw the stocky man's eyes narrow venomously, but he acted as though he had heard nothing, and the man who had laughed faced forward and said, "All right; you don't get down. But you will ride with us." He raised his right arm and gestured. "Not far, a mile or so."

This one sounded younger and his accented English was much better. But Dunaway was looking steadily at the stocky man with the gun. "You tell your friend to put the gun away," he said, without looking at the man who had laughed.

It was the third *vaquero*, a tall, lean man, who spoke. Up until now he had been an interested spectator. "You don't need the gun, Chalo." Then he said, "*Señor*, you have been expected for three days. *Mi patron* will want to hear why you are so late."

Dunaway eyed the speaker. They were obviously mistaking him for someone else, but right now that did not matter. He said, "Where is your *patron*?"

The lean man pointed to the southwest. "An hour's ride."

"To a town?"

"No, *Señor*. To the headquarters of the ranch."

Dunaway eased back a little. "Lead off," he said, because whether he had been mistaken for someone else or not, what they were talking about was shelter and he had just about abandoned any hope of finding any.

The stocky man was a centaur; one of those Mexicans bred to the saddle and who, like an

Apache, might look, and be, awkward on the ground, bandy-legged with a paunch hanging over his belt, a powerful upper body and a spindly lower body, but on the back of a horse he was where he looked best, did best, and really belonged.

As they rode with the wind pummeling them on the right side, he cast sulphurous glares at Dunaway, until Dunaway rode over close and said, "Nobody but a damned fool aims a gun at a man without cocking it."

Before the angry man could respond the lean man looked over his shoulder at him, but spoke to Dunaway. "It was a game. We have a name for it; it means someone must beg. You see?"

Dunaway considered the lean man. "I'll bet you lose a lot of friends that way."

The lean man shrugged. "Not three to one, *amigo*."

Dunaway did not yield. "Yes, even at three to one – *amigo*."

They gazed at him in what seemed to be either clinical or respectful interest, and finally the stocky man began to wag his head. Then he laughed behind his bandana, and jerked it down so that it hung loose at the throat. He had pock marks on his very dark, coarse face, and thick features, but his teeth were perfect, and that mitigated his ugliness when he smiled or laughed. "I am Gonzalo Gutierrez," he announced, all trace of his sullen anger gone.

Dunaway returned the man's look without smiling. "Then why did your friend call you Chalo?"

The stocky man blinked. "Chalo? It is the nick-name for someone named Gonzalo ... *Amigo*, where are you from – not New Mexico."

Dunaway's education had just been added to. He did not tell them where he was from. Instead, he said, "You've been watching out here for three days?"

The lean man answered. "Yes. You were supposed to be here three days ago."

Dunaway turned that over in his mind. To keep three riders out in bad weather for three days waiting to escort someone to a ranch, had to mean whoever they had been waiting for was important to someone – to their *patron*, obviously.

He said, "Bad weather, gents," and let them draw whatever conclusions they might from that. They did not seem to draw any. They had buildings in sight on the lee side of a high swale.

Dunaway looked down there and was impressed. It was a large yard with trees and a number of what appeared to be adobe-and-log structures. There was a large network of working corrals, which was interesting because Dunaway had seen no livestock all day.

The main house had red tiles on the roof and a large, covered veranda down both sides and along the front. It looked more like a mission, or perhaps the officers' quarters of some Mex army post than a residence.

There was wind-scourged smoke coming from a number of chimneys, but there was not a soul in sight in the yard as they rode in.

Inside the barn Dunaway and his bay horse had surcease from the punishing wind for the first time since daylight. It was like having a weight taken off them. The riders wordlessly went about unsaddling, so Dunaway followed their example. After the lean man had pointed to the stall for the bay horse, he pulled down his bandana and said, "My name is Carter Alvarado." Dunaway believed him. He had a complexion much lighter than his companions, although his eyes were dark. "I will take you to the house. He is waiting for you."

Dunaway finally said, "Carter, you got the wrong man."

Alvarado thought about that, then shrugged. "I don't think so. Come along."

Two:
El Patron

The room was vast and filled with very heavy, dark old carved furniture which seemed to have been made more for its richness and elaborate carving than for comfort. There was a smouldering oak-log fire in the great stone fireplace. Dunaway eyed it with interest. He had seen no oak trees.

The room had a delicate and elaborately made lamp throwing light from a pale pastel globe. The light made the room seem less ostentatious and more hospitable.

Carter Alvarado had left him at the door, and thus far no one had entered the handsome large parlour, which was more like a baronial hall than the parlour of a cow outfit. But then, maybe down in this country, which had been inhabited for several hundred years, it had been easier to accumulate wealth than it had been up north, where stockmen had only been in residence about forty years, and lived hard.

A tall, thin, older man with a full head of nearly

snow-white hair came through a doorway. He had black eyes and black brows, but his complexion was even lighter than the complexion of the half-breed Carter Alvarado.

The man nodded slowly, walked ahead and motioned toward one of the massive carved chairs. "It is bad weather," he said, going to a long, nearly black and heavily carved sideboard where he filled two gold-rimmed glasses with red wine and took one glass to Dunaway, who had remained standing. The older man smiled. "*Salud*," he said, and sipped his wine while studying his guest. Then he abruptly went to a chair near the little marble-top table with the lighted lamp upon it, sat down and continued his study.

"Please be seated," he said, and smiled again. He looked almost frail because of his thinness.

Dunaway dumped his hat beside a chair, sat down and tasted the wine. It may have been the result of his daylong punishment, or it may have been the result of his daylong hunger, but the wine tasted better than any he had ever tasted before, although admittedly Cab Dunaway did not drink much wine. Only whiskey.

"I expected you earlier," the older man said. "The weather, I suppose ..."

Dunaway was having trouble categorising his host. He did not look Mexican; maybe pure Spanish, but there was no accent to his English. He said, "My name is Cabot Dunaway."

The older man answered quietly. "I am Jaime Stuart. Jaime is Spanish for James."

Dunaway nodded. James Stuart must be another half-breed, but he certainly did not look nor sound like one. Cab said, "Mister Stuart, I ran across three of your men. They threw down on me. Then we came here. My guess is that they were expecting someone, but it sure as hell wasn't me. I've never been south of Raton before in my life, never saw any of you before, and didn't even know there was a ranch down here."

The older man lifted his glass. He was clearly an individual who enjoyed good wine. He seemed to be reviewing what he had just heard. Then he showed that soft, small smile again. "Tell me, Mister Dunaway – have you ever been in Albuquerque?"

"No sir, never have."

"Nor heard of a man named Frank Baxter, who is also known as *el Leoncito*, the little lion?"

"Nope. I'm sorry to disappoint you, but I've never heard of anyone called a little lion, or Frank Baxter. Once, I knew a Charley Baxter, but that was over in Idaho. He was the rangeboss for the cow outfit I worked for one season."

Without warning Carter Alvarado came soundlessly through a doorway and without looking at Cab Dunaway, went over to lean and whisper into the ear of Jaime Stuart. Then he turned, still without looking at Dunaway, and went back the way he had come. Dunaway watched him depart, and speculated that Alvarado had been just beyond that doorway, eavesdropping.

Stuart drained his glass and put it aside. He said, "Would you like your glass re-filled, Mister Dunaway?"

Cabot hadn't emptied the glass. "No thanks. But it's very fine wine."

"We make it here on the ranch. We are almost a self-sufficient unit, Mister Dunaway."

Cab could believe it, after seeing all those little buildings around the yard.

"That has been the custom down here for a long time," explained the older man. "It started because when the Spanish settled this country there were no towns so each ranch had to be able to provide whatever it needed. Some of the people here were here when my father was alive ... Well ... it has been very hard to keep ranches like this one together. We are not very far from the Mexican border. We lose cattle and horses, and I could show you our ranch cemetery. We have also lost many people to cattle and horse thieves, to marauders and *pronunciados* up out of Mexico ... And the other people who are in the country now. The *yanquis*." James Stuart stopped speaking and looked steadily at Cab Dunaway.

Cab drained his glass, put it aside and spread his hands. "Mister, I've never been in this country before."

Stuart's fixed gaze softened. "I was expecting Frank Baxter. I sent a man to him up in Durham with two hundred dollars in gold."

Cab had no idea who Frank Baxter was, but he had some experience with human nature. If someone handed a man two hundred dollars in gold, especially if he was someone with a nickname like the little lion, there was an excellent chance that the man would never arrive, or, if he did arrive, he'd be bleary-eyed with shaking hands and a monumental headache.

Stuart was watching Dunaway's face. "You think I made a mistake?"

Cab smiled. "Maybe. You wanted to hire him as your rangeboss?"

"No. Carter Alvarado, one of the men you met, is my *mayordomo*. There is not a better one. No ... Mister Dunaway, you made Chalo Gutierrez back down when his gun was aimed at you."

Cabot gazed at the frail-appearing man thinking that this was what Alvarado had whispered in his ear. "He wasn't going to shoot me, Mister Stuart. If you figure to shoot someone you cock your gun when you aim it."

James Stuart hung fire before speaking again. "Do you mind telling me whether you have ever hired out to someone to use your gun?"

Dunaway did not mind answering. "No, I never have ... Is that what Frank Baxter does?"

"Yes."

"I see. So you were expecting a gunman when I came along." Cab leaned to arise from the chair. Standing and looking down at the older man he said, "Next time, just summons them; don't send 'em the money in advance."

"No," replied James Stuart from his chair. "That was not the pay. That was only to get him interested. I intend to pay much more – in gold, Mister Dunaway." James Stuart arose and took his little glass to the sideboard and with Dunaway watching, he refilled it, then turned. "One more glass?"

Dunaway shook his head. "No thanks. What I'd like, though, is permission to bed down in your barn until this wind stops. Maybe until the morning. And maybe you could tell me where there is a town called Matanzas."

Stuart was quiet again for a long time, then he answered. "Matanzas is about five miles southeast. That was your destination?"

"Yes. There is a man down there I rode with a long time ago. Sam Cutler. He wrote me a letter a year ago inviting me down. He bought a saloon in Matanzas."

Stuart put his glass aside untouched. "He is dead."

Cab blinked.

"He was a friend of mine, Mister Dunaway. Right here in this room we spent a lot of winter nights visiting; sometimes playing pedro and drinking wine. He was shot in the back of the head while he was facing away from his bar."

Dunaway slowly leaned to retrieve his hat. He needed a little time and James Stuart gave him all he needed before speaking again. "Who shot him?"

"No one knows," replied the older man with a slight shrug. "When you've been to Matanzas you'll understand. Over the last year a lot of men have been killed."

"There was a reason, Mister Stuart."

Again the older man made that slight shrug. He went over to adjust the small lamp because darkness was seeping in. When he straightened around he said, "You were a rangeman. A tophand?"

"Yes."

"Tophands make a good wage, Mister Dunaway. Only a foreman makes more. I will pay you five times as much as you would make as a foreman."

Cab Dunaway stared at the frail, older man. "Let me ask you something: what is this all about?"

"Over the last four months I have lost many cattle and horses. As nearly as Carter can figure it, in the neighbourhood of a thousand head of cattle and about three hundred horses ... I only raise blooded horses and I only keep up-graded, quality cattle ... The reason my men were waiting for Frank Baxter was that I was told by a friend from south of Matanzas that I am to be killed."

"Who by?"

"It is hearsay, Mister Dunaway. By Seth Wolf, the man who has moved into Matanzas. I would guess he had Sam Cutler killed. Since he arrived with his Texans cattle and horses have disappeared from all the ranches, and people have been shot the way Sam was – when their backs were turned."

"And you wanted Baxter to kill Wolf."

James Stuart nodded his head at the same moment a furious gust of wind struck the house, which had walls three feet thick. The windows rattled and wind whipping across the red-tiled roof made a forlorn wailing sound.

Dunaway did not speak again until the noise had gone. Then he said, "How many Texans?"

"I'm not sure. Some of my friends have said fifteen. Among my riders who have kinsmen in Matanzas, it is an army of them."

Dunaway considered his old hat while holding it in both hands. "Is the army down here?"

James Stuart showed a mirthless grin. "Yes. At Fort McDowell, sixty miles south and east. The border is patrolled from their fort."

"Why haven't you sent for them?"

"I have. Three different times. I get back no answers to my letters ... Mister Dunaway, I sent my daughter to her aunt up in Durham. I know what you will think when I say it, but for the past few weeks my riders see strangers on my land. They have seen them on the little hills watching this yard, this house. It has grown steadily worse. Three days ago they tried to catch Chalo Gutierrez. They chased him almost back to the yard and fired at him ... I am besieged. I don't know Seth Wolf. I wouldn't know the man if he stepped through that door, but this much I *do* know: he is going to own this ranch and everything that goes with it. Why my ranch, I don't know, except that it is the largest one in the Matanzas territory, and my livestock is the result of four generations of up-breeding by my family."

Dunaway dropped the hat atop his head. "Mister Stuart, Frank Baxter wouldn't be able to help you. No single, solitary individual would be able to. You need the army. At the very least, if all this is true, you need at least a company of hired gunfighters." He and the older man stood gazing at one another, then Cab turned toward the door. "Can't you hire some Mexicans from south of the border?"

"I told you, *amigo*, we are under siege. They have been tightening their surround for several weeks."

Cab turned with his hand on the latch. "Well, if Sam is dead then I made a long ride for nothing. But as long as I'm down here, I guess I can ride over and find that soldier-fort for you."

Stuart strolled over and held the door for his guest. They went out upon the roofed-over wide veranda where it was possible to see a number of lights among the buildings around the yard. Stuart said, "You are welcome to use the bunkhouse with the other men. I will ask Carter to have food sent to you."

"No thanks. I'll bed down near my horse. And I've got a little grub in my saddlebags."

James Stuart brushed Dunaway's arm as the younger man started toward the pair of wide, low steps leading down from the veranda. When Cab turned the older man spoke quietly.

"You can't reach Fort McDowell. I don't think you will even be able to leave my yard in the morning, or, if they let you ride out, they will run you down and kill you ... They will know you rode in today."

Dunaway squinted at the older man. A few hours ago he had been willing to take any protection from the storm he could get, and he had found it, and now he was being told he was a prisoner of men he did not know, had not even heard of until an hour or so ago, and that they would kill him if he attempted to leave.

He said, "Good night," and left the older man standing on the veranda watching him buck the sharp little gusts of wind all the way to the barn.

In there, as at the big main-house, the wind could not make much of an impression because the building had immensely thick mud walls. But it whistled down through the runway.

Still, it was no longer blowing steadily. There were erratic interludes when it did not blow at all, followed by fresh gusts coming from different directions. He returned to the doorway to study the sky for some sign that the storm would blow itself out before morning.

Without any warning a body of riders charged into the yard from the east. He heard them moments before he could see their eerie silhouettes, then the gunfire started and Dunaway instinctively jumped back away from the barn opening.

The horsemen circled the big yard at a lope firing through windows, into doors, even down through the barn where Dunaway had to dive for cover. Some of them were using handguns, some were firing carbines. He could occasionally hear carbine mechanisms jerking back and forth as the wild riders flipped their Winchesters with one hand to get a fresh cartridge into the chamber.

The noise was deafening. Bullets peeled wood inside the barn and struck solidly into adobe walls. Finally, the riders concentrated on the main-house. Dunaway could hear them over there. It sounded like a battle except that all the gunfire was coming from one direction.

Then they wheeled, threw more lead into the buildings around the yard and spurred in a dead run back eastward in the direction from which they had come.

Three:
The Dead And The Living

For a long while after the marauders had attacked there was not a sound in the yard, nor were the lights, which had been burning before the raid, still glowing. Only the smell of burnt gunpowder lingered.

Some broken glass falling made a musical sound, and the horses, which had been agitated during the attack, still milled in diminishing fright.

Dunaway picked up his hat, struck his leg with it, put it on and went up to the front barn doorway. The yard, all the buildings, including the main-house, were like tombs. The only indication that there had been gunfire was a small dead dog over near one of the adobe *jacals* where the ranch retainers lived.

Then the keening, high wail of a woman broke the stillness. It rose and fell, like an Indian chant. Dunaway placed the sound without difficulty. Across from him and slightly southward, not far from the dead dog, a riddled wooden doorway hung slack on broken hinges. The wailing was coming from over there.

As he stood motionless a lean shadow hurried out of another *jacal* and disappeared beyond the broken door. He had recognised the silhouette as belonging to Carter Alvarado. After a while the wailing ceased. Only an occasional moan lingered in its wake.

Dunaway walked toward the main-house. Its front wall looked like the Alamo must have looked after its thirteen-day siege by Santa Anna's Mexican army. Clearly the marauders had intended to do the most damage over there, and they had succeeded. The solitary large glass window in the front wall had a few dagger-like shards of glass still in the frame, otherwise the glass was completely gone. The door too, for all its massive, oaken strength, had been broken at the top hinge and sagged heavily as Dunaway moved to enter the house. It was much heavier than he anticipated. He had to grunt to lift it wide enough so that he could slip through.

The large parlour was a shambles. The elegant little filagreed lamp which he had seen atop its marble-top table had been knocked over beyond a nearby chair, its coal oil spreading like dark water in all directions. A few pieces of furniture had escaped damage but everything else had been riddled.

Dunaway's eyes were accustomed to the gloom, but he knew that, come daylight, this room was going to look much worse than it did in darkness.

He started across in the direction of the doorway through which James Stuart had appeared yesterday at their first meeting, stopped before entering what appeared to be a hallway beyond, and gazed upon the man lying face-up, feet and lower legs in the parlour, the rest of him in the hallway.

Dunaway knelt. He did not need light. Perhaps Stuart had been sitting in his parlour, possibly reading, or having a glass of wine before retiring, no one would ever know. But he had certainly made a dash for the hallway, and had been hit at least eight times perhaps before he reached the doorway.

Dunaway stood up and rolled a smoke which he placed between his lips then neglected to light. James Stuart looked even more frail in death, and in the poor light.

Dunaway turned back and left the house to stand upon the veranda. Now there were a few lights among the buildings, but even as he stood there all but two of them were abruptly blocked out by people placing blankets over their windows.

He spat. That was a useless precaution. The marauders would not return.

A frog-like shadow moved from the edge of the house with a drawn gun, edged closer and when Dunaway quietly said, "Put that damned gun away," the shadow slumped slightly, then obeyed. He turned on the thick, mis-shapen silhouette in annoyance. "What in the hell do you think you're doing? They're gone. Come up here on the porch."

It was Chalo Gutierrez, sweating although it was not a warm night. He spoke Spanish. "Mother of

God, may their souls forever burn."

Dunaway had followed only the first part of it, but he needed no interpretation. He reached and tapped Gutierrez on his barrel chest. "When I'm around speak English." Then he saw pale shadows moving among the *jacals* and asked what had happened down there. Gutierrez answered in his guttural English.

"The man who was with us today when we met you, Diego Elizondo ... they killed him and his little boy, and his old mother. And their dog."

Dunaway finally lighted the cigarette and gazed down where the floating white silhouettes moved in and out. He did not know the man's name, he only recalled that he had laughed easily and had been pleasant. "Who else?"

Chalo Gutierrez turned his columnar neck as far as it would go. "*El Patron*?"

"Yes. Who else?"

Chalo looked upwards. "Three people wounded. Another child may die and a pregnant woman. She was hit through the hips."

Dunaway dropped his smoke and ground it savagely underfoot. "Who were they, Chalo?"

Gutierrez spread very thick, broad hands with stubby fingers, and muttered something that sounded like 'yo no say,' and saw Dunaway's head coming around slowly. "I don't know, *Señor* ... I was in bed. I was sleeping hard. I had some mescal with my supper, so I was sleeping like the dead ... I had a hard time awakening. You understand?"

What Cab Dunaway understood was that Chalo

Gutierrez had not answered his question but had spent time justifying or excusing himself for not being capable of fighting back. Dunaway stepped over and leaned on a porch upright. If Chalo felt guilty, there would be plenty of that sentiment to go around, but how do people anticipate a vicious and sudden attack by mounted gunmen? They don't. He said, "Go find Alvarado and tell him I'm here on the porch and want to see him. Then go find out how many people were hit or killed, and come back here. All right?"

Chalo considered the leaning man's profile, nodded his head and went down off the veranda and across the yard in an ungainly lope.

Dunaway had never seen anything like that attack. He had never been in the army nor taken part in any posse actions. Perhaps that, and what Chalo had told him about the dead people, and those who might die, were what kept him leaning like a stone until Carter Alvarado walked up, hatless and carrying a carbine. Dunaway looked at the gun. "Did you use it?" he asked coldly. Alvarado leaned the Winchester aside, sensing the other man's icy mood, and did not answer. Of course he had not used it. Like everyone else he was caught asleeep in bed. By the time he groped in darkness for his britches and the gun, the raiders were racing out of the yard.

"*Señor* ..."

Dunaway turned his head slightly to regard the lean man with a sulphurous look. "My name is Cab Dunaway, not *señor*, you understand? And no more

Spanish." He did not allow the foreman to reply. "Mister Stuart told me tonight they were going to kill him."

Alvarado glanced slowly in the direction of the broken oaken door and the darkness beyond it, but remained silent as Dunaway continued to speak.

"They did it. He's in there with holes in him everywhere but in his head. He also told me they've been running off his livestock. Well ...?"

"It is true. Hundreds of horses and cattle." Alvarado looked down across the yard because he did not like to look at the face of the *gringo*. "We went after them many times."

"And?"

"We lost some men, *Señor*, and down near Matanzas the tracks had been overlayed with other tracks."

"Who were they, Carter?"

Alvarado brought his eyes back slowly. "Texans. That's all I know."

"Tell me why your *patron* didn't fight back?"

Alvarado looked steadily into Dunaway's face when he said, "How do you fight the wind? How do you stop a landslide?"

"At least you try, Carter."

Alvarado nodded his head slightly as though this might have been his own private opinion. "You didn't know *el patron*. He was a very kindly and gentle man."

"Yeah. And for that, he's lying in there on his back with blood all over him ... How many riders do you have?"

"Riders? Nine, counting me." Alvarado's dark eyes were like wet obsidian as he stared at Dunaway. He thought he knew what was coming.

"All right. You go round them up, every man with carbines and handguns, and plenty of ammunition for both." Dunaway returned the wide-eyed look. "Carter, I'm not a kindly nor a gentle man."

"*Señor*, they will be back in their town. It's like a fortress." Alvarado paused. "It belongs to them now. None of us have even ridden close to Matanzas since ..."

"Carter, among those nine men, how many are cowards?"

Alvarado spread work-roughened hands. "None, *Señor*, but –"

"I'm going to tell you for the last time my name is not *señor* ... Maybe they're back in their town. Maybe not. We're going to find out – right now, tonight – while they think everyone out here is wailing over their dead and pounding ashes in their hair. You go get those men over to the barn for horses. I don't care a damn how they protest, get them over there if you have to use your gun, *sabe usted*?"

The *mayordomo* nodded slowly but made no move to depart. He was looking into the darkness beyond the broken oaken door again. Carter Alvarado, like everyone else on the big ranch, had taken orders from only one man most of his life. Carter was no different from the others tonight; he was pained, bewildered, but right now he was, most of all, utterly confused and demoralised. He had thought his *patron* would have survived. Since boyhood he had known James Stuart, and it took a long time for a man like Alvarado to accept something as cataclysmic as the death of his *patron*. It meant the end of Alvarado's orderly existence. He turned slowly from looking into the dark parlour and nodded his head, then went slowly down to the yard and trudged across it, with Dunaway watching him.

There was a chill in the air, which indicated that it was later than Dunaway had thought. He pushed up off the porch-post, regarded the broken door for a moment, then left the porch and was intercepted on his way to the barn by Chalo Gutierrez, whose face looked even sweatier now in soft-sad starlight than it had formerly looked.

"Four are now dead," he said. "The pregnant woman died a little while ago. She bled to death. Nothing could be done. There are six with wounds." Having ended his report Chalo flopped both arms in a gesture of resignation.

Dunaway considered the pock-marked, very dark and ugly face. "Get your carbine, plenty of bullets, then get down to the barn and saddle a horse."

Gutierrez's eyes sprung wide open. "What are you going to do?"

"Not me, all of us. We're going after them."

Chalo flopped both arms again. "In the darkness? They will be back at Matanzas and if we go anywhere near, they will know it and ambush us, *Señor*."

"For the last time, I'm not *señor*."

Chalo nodded his head. "Cab," he said. "*Pardona mi*. There are many of them. We are one man less now that Elizondo is dead ... Eight of us, counting Carter Alvarado."

"Nine, counting me. Do as I said, get your guns and meet the rest of us at the barn. And Chalo – this time if you aim your damned sixgun, cock it."

Dunaway continued toward the barn, while behind him in the centre of the yard the bandy-legged, frog-like dark man stared after him. It would, he thought, be suicide. It was an insane thing to even think about. Nine of them going up against only God knew how many of Seth Wolf's thieves and murderers.

Chalo had a jug of tequila under the bed in his little house. He turned to cross toward the *jacal*. He would get his guns and extra bullets, but for this kind of absolute madness a man needed something more. He paused out front of his house and gazed at the sky. Every star was showing. The weather should be as it had been, now that the cursed wind had departed, which meant he had better also take along a poncho because within another four hours or so when dawn arrived it would be as cold as the bosom of a witch.

He entered the low doorway muttering to himself as he groped for the candle which should have been on a rickety table, but which had fallen to the floor, or had been knocked there by a stray bullet. He had buried many friends, and a few enemies, in their ponchos.

He found the jug but never did find the broken candle. He drank deeply, re-stoppered the jug and put it carefully back in its dark place, then he groped in darkness for his Winchester in its boot, his extra bullets and his poncho. It was a fairly new poncho with horizontal red and green stripes. A very nice poncho to be buried in. That *gringo* was crazy. They would all be equally crazy if they rode with him tonight. He knew they would refuse to do that, nevertheless he left the *jacal* carrying his saddlegun and poncho.

Someone had hung a smoky old lantern aloft in the barn. Its meagre light was better than no light. As Chalo appeared in the doorway a rider turned and said, "Hurry up," in Spanish.

They were all there saddling and bridling animals. Obviously, no one had refused. Chalo marched down through to find a horse out back in the corrals. They were a bunch of *loco cabezas*, a bunch of crazy heads.

The tequila warmed him. It even brought on a somewhat benign attitude as he led the caught-horse back inside to be saddled. He knew them all. Had known them since he had been a young man. Besides, when they were all buried he alone among them would have the most resplendent poncho.

The crazy heads with salt on their backs!

Four:
The Creek Beyond The Boulders

Dunaway was riding beside Alvarado when he asked where the cattle were, and Carter, expecting almost any question but that one, raised an arm to gesture with. "West of here. We drove most of them over there because when they were on the south range, that was where the thieves raided."

"All of them?"

"No. There are three thousand – well, at one time there were three thousand cows. Over to the west there may be a thousand head. The others are wet cows; we always keep them many miles northward because up there the grass is strong." Alvarado rested his hand atop the saddlehorn and gazed at his companion. "This is not the way to Matanzas."

They were riding west. Dunaway's reply was a grunt.

The men watched him up in the lead with Carter Alvarado and in muted voices discussed his rough, hard-fisted manner. Chalo, whose mood was by now almost happy, put into words what the others had not. "If *el patron* is dead, along with the others, then we will follow this one. Comrades, we will always follow someone, will we not? I think this is crazy, but I would like to believe it isn't. And besides, there are the dead. Certainly?"

No one took it up.

Alvarado was silent until in the dusky distance he could discern a stand of cottonwood trees, which were a landmark he had known since early manhood. "Beyond another mile; they will have spread out, but they will —" He stopped in mid-sentence. They all halted and sat listening. Cows do not bawl much at night, like almost everything else, they sleep. There were bawling cows up ahead somewhere, invisible in the darkness. To the seasoned ears of the motionless riders, those sounds were being made by distressed cattle. Nor was it likely that wolves would have got so many cows upset.

Alvarado turned and stared at Dunaway. "How did you know?"

Dunaway did not answer. He was listening, fixing in his mind from which direction the animals were bawling. They were moving. He spat and asked what was southward. Alvarado explained that it was perhaps three, four hundred miles of semi-desert country.

"How far is the Mex border?" Dunaway asked, and Alvarado shook his head. "Too far. They wouldn't take them that far. They wouldn't have to. They might even sell them to the stockmen up by Durham and down here to the eastward where there are other towns and big ranches."

"What I'm trying to guess," Dunaway explained, "is which direction they will be going."

Alvarado did not consider that a mystery. "They are going south now. But there is nothing down there. They will turn left or right. East or west."

Dunaway was lifting his reinhand when he said, "Which, left or right?"

Alvarado scowled, "I don't know. They would know but none of us would."

Dunaway twisted in the saddle. "Chalo; if they catch you they'll kill you. Remember that. Now go down there and spy on them. If they turn, come back. And don't take all night. You understand?"

Chalo loped away, grinning. The others watched him until he was nothing more than a faint sound of shod hooves. Dunaway dismounted them for the wait. A young *vaquero* laughed and said he did not believe Chalo would be able to find his way back in the dark, because he had been drinking.

But the young rangeman was wrong, Chalo came back in an easy lope the same way he had departed, and although he was not smiling when he swung to the ground, it was clear that his mood was still very good.

He held up his rein-hand. "They are going west now."

"How many riders?" Dunaway asked, and Chalo finally smiled.

"*Jefe*, you told me they would kill me. I didn't

count them. I didn't get that close. What I saw was two men in the drag, but there were others up ahead because I could hear them swearing at the cattle."

Dunaway turned on Alvarado. "What lies west of here?"

Carter Alvarado was beginning to suspect what Dunaway had in mind. "The farther west you go, the rougher the country becomes. There are trees and some big rocks, as high as a mounted man, and black. There are deep arroyos and ... Do you want to ambush them?"

"That's the idea."

Alvarado saw the looks on the faces of the men standing around them. He shrugged. "If we ride hard for an hour. They can't drive cattle very fast. I will show you."

As they mounted up Alvarado loped ahead. The others followed him. A grey and grizzled *vaquero* was riding with Dunaway. He was silent a long time, until they had Alvarado in sight on ahead, then he spoke.

"*Señor*, it would not have happened if the *patron*'s father had been alive. He knew how to take care of renegades. He shot them."

Cab said nothing. He waited until they were up with Alvarado, then asked why he had stopped. The *mayordomo* pointed. "Three miles from here there is a wide field of big stones. The Indians used to camp there because there is a spring, and —"

"Never mind the damned Indians. What about this boulder field; can we ambush them up there?"

Alvarado lowered his arm and considered the face of the man who had spoken. He nodded just once. "If they go anywhere near that place, we can ambush them ... Cab; what happens if we are successful? It won't be all of Wolf's band, and when he learns what happened out here ..."

Dunaway was nudging his horse when he said, "If you waste time about what's going to happen next week, you'll sure lose a lot of working time now, won't you?"

Because Alvarado did not take them directly to the boulder field, they were almost two full hours getting up there, and the distance was only about three miles. He led them northward, far up and around, then back down so that when they saw the huge stones they were approaching them from the west.

Now, the noise of agitated cows was louder, and the smell of cattle was strong. But they could see nothing.

Dunaway rode to the edge of the hundred-acre site where some momentous event in pre-historic times had caused all those huge rocks to be flung down where there were no rocks like them, or rocks of that size, for many miles.

But there were trees on this west range. Dunaway took the lead from this point on, and Carter dropped back to ride beside that grizzled older *vaquero.* They scarcely spoke.

Dunaway went into the boulder field, his bay horse picking its way because, aside from the very large and massive rocks, the ground was strewn with much smaller stones.

He rode directly toward the sound of cattle, and stopped when a man's hooting shout came distinctly up to him. The driven cattle, by Dunaway's estimate, were a good half-mile south of the boulder field. A young rider walked his horse up and halted, facing toward the sound. By starlight he looked pleased.

Dunaway did not reflect upon how some men might derive pleasure from doing something like they were out here to do. He was studying the ground ahead. The grass was not very tall, and it was green. But unless it could have been fifteen feet tall it would not have offered shelter as they stalked the cattle thieves.

He said, "All right. Let's go west another mile." The younger man immediately turned his horse. What had been proposed was not at all involved; simply catch the thieves out in the open and ambush them. The *vaquero* had never seen this kind of a fight and was eager now to do so. Dunaway watched him for a moment, then wagged his head. He had never seen this kind of an action before either, but he was far from pleased over its prospects.

They loped to cover the ground swiftly. Alvarado came up to Dunaway and said, "If they keep on this way, they will pass Sangre Creek. The cattle will want water. But the creek is another mile onward."

Dunaway nodded. "Then you lead the way to the creek." He liked this idea because it would allow them even more time to get into position.

Sangre Creek was roughly two miles in advance of the driven herd, so although their bawling was audible, it was only faintly so.

When they were dismounting Dunaway studied the sky. There was no moon and out along the uneven horizon a soft, blue paleness was firming up. He took his horse back from the creek and left it tied as the others had done, then he returned to the crossing carrying his saddlegun, and his coat. It was cold.

They had a long wait ahead of them. Cattle ordinarily did not walk more than three or four miles an hour. Driven cattle might do a little better, but as the men worked their way out of sight into the willows along Sangre Creek, they knew there would be plenty of time to establish a good ambush.

That old *vaquero* did not assume command so much as he pointedly offered advice about this matter. As Dunaway listened to him, and watched the stringy arms gesture, he had the impression that the older man had done this before.

There was very little talk. Ordinarily rangemen in this kind of a situation, with time to waste, had comments to make. These men had left their dead back in the ranch yard.

Alvarado strolled over where Dunaway was sitting on soft earth like a bronco Indian, listening for any change in the direction of the drive, and squatted down with his carbine up-ended to lean upon.

"I worry about this," he said candidly. "You

don't know these men."

Dunaway neither spoke nor looked around. The sounds were getting closer by the minute.

"If any of them are hurt ..."

Dunaway finally turned his head. "They better be hurt, and in the first blast, because it seemed to me back there a ways there was a lot of them."

Alvarado said, "What then?"

"What do you mean – what then?"

"Wolf will come to the ranch with an army. He has killed people over around Matanzas for nothing; just for being slow in allowing his men to rob their houses and run off their livestock."

Dunaway turned aside to expectorate, then did not look at his companion, but peered eastward toward the oncoming sound of the cattle. "What do you think we ought to do? Ride back and bury your dead and keep inside the yard?"

Alvarado did not speak again for a long time. He too was listening to the oncoming drive. When he finally did speak, it was about something altogether different, making it seem to Dunaway that he was embarrassed about what he had said before.

"Those will be the steers and dry cows we put on the west range. There were some wet cows with them, but in the darkness by now they will have cut back to find their calves. It's impossible to drive wet cows in broad daylight if their calves aren't with them. In the dark ..." he shrugged.

Dunaway neither knew nor cared which variety of cattle the thieves were driving toward him. "You better go make damned sure our horses are tied good, because when the firing starts those damned cattle are going to stampede every which way. We don't want to end up out here on foot."

Alvarado arose slowly to obey. "They will stampede back the way they came," he said, and walked away.

Dunaway waited fifteen minutes longer, then arose and went among the willows to see how the old *vaquero* had placed the riders. The old man himself was standing beside a lightning-struck cottonwood tree which had no top. He nodded to Dunaway. "It will be over in five minutes," he said, holding his old saddlegun in the bend of one arm.

Dunaway nodded and walked on past. The riders were strung out among the willows on both sides of a gravelly wide ford. The creek was deeper than it looked where it was closely confined within its banks, but where the ford was, it was much wider, and therefore quite shallow. It was muddy, so evidently the horses had stirred silt when someone had led them down to drink.

Chalo Gutierrez showed handsome white teeth in his villainous face when Dunaway came up. Chalo's load of liquor had to a great extent evaporated. "I think the cattle will take care of the ones we don't shoot, *amigo*. Did you ever see a man and his horse when a herd of cattle got them down and stampeded over them?"

Dunaway had seen such a sight. "A couple of times. Tell me something, Chalo. How can a man like Wolf take over a whole town?"

Chalo's malevolent smile widened. "If they are

afraid of him, he can do it. In Mexico it is done all the time by *bandeleros*, and even the army."

"This isn't Mexico."

"*Amigo*, human nature is the same everywhere. If you have enough men with you who kill people and point their guns at you ... People who live in towns are different." Chalo turned with his head cocked. The cattle drive was coming directly toward his hiding place. They had probably smelled water. Dunaway slapped Gutierrez on the back. "Be careful," he said, and turned to go back to the position he had chosen for himself.

Earlier, he had wanted a smoke. Now, the idea was not in his thoughts at all. Instead, he was considering something Carter Alvarado had said: After this fight, what came next? .

Only one thing could come next.

Dunaway lifted the carbine, examined its sliding action, counted the loads in its magazine and chamber, squatted down leaning on it, and waited for something to move in front of him.

There would probably be a point rider. It was not mandatory, but it helped driven cattle to move in the proper direction by offering them something to sight on.

If there was a point rider, he was very shortly now going to look like James Stuart had looked; shot all to hell with his drying eyes staring straight upwards.

Dunaway spat, dried wet palms on his jacket, and re-gripped the carbine. What in the hell was he doing here? He owed none of these people anything, hadn't even known them until yesterday.

He thought briefly of his old friend Sam Cutler, who had been shot in the head when his back was turned. He also recalled the desolate wailing of that woman back in the ranch yard. And Elizondo, the man who had laughed yesterday when Dunaway had faced Chalo Gutierrez down when he'd had his sixgun aimed directly at Dunaway.

Finally, he thought of *el patron*, the frail, kindly man who hadn't really known how to fight back, and had sent for just one gunfighter.

Finally, he saw faint movement ahead and slightly on his left. Well; whatever in hell he was doing here, it was now too late to be anywhere else. He raised his carbine, snugged it back and cocked it.

Five:
Toward Daylight

But Dunaway did not get off the first shot. He was taking plenty of time because he wanted the targets to be well in sight, when north of him a carbine flashed orange light and that point rider went off his horse as though swept away by an invisible hand.

Then, as the lead cattle pulled back in surprise and fright, other horsemen spurred ahead yelling at the leaders. They did not act as though they had heard that gunshot. Dunaway sighed. They had it coming; they had killed women and others back in the yard, but this was like shooting crows. He found another target, and this time every saddlegun along the creek blazed. Dunaway's target was already falling when he fired.

Now, the cattle were terrified. They did as Alvarado had predicted, they ran blind in all directions, but the main body turned upon those in back and using great weight began crowding and shoving until those cattle also turned back the way they had come. The stampede was under way, noise, dust, rank smell and all.

Men were yelling at one another and trying to use the great tide of red backs as camouflage as they too fled eastward. They were Seth Wolf's survivors, and what Dunaway had feared did not occur. Those rustlers fired from the saddle, shooting blindly. Perhaps the panic of the cattle was transmittable to the humans. Whether it was or not, with Dunaway's riders still firing, the rustlers fled.

The old *vaquero* had been wrong. It hadn't taken five minutes. More like two minutes. Someone south of Dunaway's position continued to fire until his gun was shot out. Dunaway thought that probably had been that warlike younger rider.

It was over almost as quickly as it had started. They remained among the creek-willows, listening to distant outcries, the clicking sound of many horns striking among cattle who were running in a big crowd, and finally with those sounds growing less strident, a man called out, his words indistinguishable but his outcry close. Dunaway stood up and gazed out where the attack had occurred. He expected to see dead horses but there were none, which probably was unique under the circumstances. That old *vaquero* came up without a sound and said, "I think *Señor* Wolf won't have too many men from now on." He looked at Dunaway, then started walking in the direction of that man who had cried out.

Dunaway followed. The others, with those two examples, also walked away from the creek.

Dunaway counted them. It had been a complete success, they had not lost a man. That actually did not surprise him. If ever men had been caught completely off-guard, those cattle thieves had.

Carter Alvarado was ahead and with the others watching, he hung his carbine low and cocked it. When they all got up there, Alvarado spoke without taking his eyes off the man sitting on the ground fifteen feet ahead. "Prisoners? What can we do with prisoners?"

No one answered him. There were four dead men and the living one sitting dazed under Carter's gun. Chalo and the old *vaquero* went about systematically collecting weapons. They would also have taken pocket-watches, money, spurs and belt-buckles except that they thought Dunaway would be angry. That young rider was standing in one place looking steadily at the first of the dead cattle thieves he had come upon, and now his expression was different.

Dunaway considered the dazed man. He did not see any blood. The man was in his thirties and had a square-jawed face with wide-spaced eyes. He needed a shave and a shearing. Dunaway leaned, tossed the man's handgun away and said, "Get up."

The rustler obeyed, but he was a little unsteady on his feet as he looked from Carter to Cab Dunaway. He did not open his mouth. Dunaway got the impression the rustler knew the men who had ridden with Dunaway, and who were now congregating around the prisoner. He looked very unsure as he swung his gaze to Dunaway.

"What's your name?" Cab asked, and got a strained reply. "John Rose." Dunaway waited to speak again until Alvarado had eased the hammer down on his saddlegun and had grounded the weapon. "Do you know the names of these dead men?"

"Yes. That one is —"

"I don't care what their names are," stated Dunaway, looking steadily at John Rose. "You know what happens to cattle thieves?"

Rose knew but he did not speak, he stood looking at Dunaway, then he said, "Who are you?"

Dunaway ignored the question. "You killed a pregnant woman tonight, John. And a little kid. And an old woman."

John Rose had almost no chance to see the dawn and he knew it, but he had to try, so he raised a soiled sleeve to mop his face as he spoke. "Not me, mister. There were fifteen riders. I was just one out of fifteen. I —"

A man cocking his sixgun behind Rose stopped the flow of words. He was no longer dazed; every instinct and nerve in his body was straining. But the bullet did not come, nor had Cab expected it to; yesterday these same *vaqueros* had used the same trick on him, only no one had cocked a gun. Dunaway glanced over Rose's shoulder. It was the old *vaquero* with the cocked gun. Cab said, "Put it away," and the older man obeyed, then made a bitter smile.

Dunaway asked what had happened to Rose. When the first volley of gunfire had erupted Rose's horse had started to buck. Rose had been thrown and had landed on his head. He had been knocked unconscious.

Dunaway told the young rider to search the man. They all watched as the *vaquero* tossed aside a wicked-bladed boot-knife and a stubby under-and-over derringer from a pocket. Dunaway said, "Mister, we're goin' to load your friends, and you're goin' to lead us to Matanzas."

John Rose thought a moment, then said, "All right, but I don't want to be out in front."

"That's where you'll be, John."

Rose stared at Dunaway. "I don't know who you are, mister, but I know one thing: You ain't been to Matanzas lately. Those fellers who got away – they'll get back to town long before we do. If Wolf don't round up everyone and come out lookin' for you, he'll have Matanzas ready and waiting. He's got a lot of guns down there, mister."

Dunaway turned aside to address the riders. "Put those dead ones behind your saddles and let's get to riding." He looked at the old *vaquero*. "You take this buzzard-bait up behind you, and if he even shifts his weight, kill him."

The men went after their horses leaving Rose facing Cab Dunaway. The outlaw showed no expression. "Mister, you're goin' to get a lot of beaners killed if you go down there."

"You among them," stated Dunaway. "But I'll give you a choice; the first tree we come to we can hang you for rustling cattle. Or you can figure out a way for us to get into Wolf's town."

Rose put all his weight on one hip and eyed Dunaway closely. "You're crazy, mister. It can't be done."

"Then we'll hang you and that'll be one less burden on our horses."

"I'll show you a way that might work," stated the outlaw somewhat quickly.

"I hope it's a good way, John, because they will be in front of you and we'll be behind you. If you get us trapped – if they don't kill you, we will."

Rose raised a hand to his head, rubbing his temple, which may have been the unconscious movement of a man who had landed on his head, or it may have indicated his quandary.

The old *vaquero* led up Dunaway's bay horse and as Cab was accepting the reins he asked in Spanish what the *vaquero*'s name was. The old man broadly smiled; to him, this was an indication that he had been noticed. "Onix Cepeda, *Jefe*."

"Be careful of this son of a bitch, Onix," Dunaway said, and stepped past to watch the bodies being flung over horses' rumps as the other riders stoically did a job no one liked.

By the time they were riding again, the cold was particularly noticeable, and Carter Alvarado came up beside Dunaway to point toward the horizon. "It's a long ride. It will be broad daylight when we get down there."

Dunaway had already noticed the slight change in the amount of light, as well as the pre-dawn cold. He rolled and lit a smoke before replying to Alvarado. "You get better targets in daylight, Carter."

Alvarado's brow dropped. "We don't have enough men, Cab. You can't make war against a man like Seth Wolf like this. He will massacre us. He has almost an army down there."

"These bastards would have massacred us too, if they'd had the chance, Carter. What we need is another surprise."

"How? You heard that man. At least eight or ten got away from here. They'll be back in Matanzas getting the place stirred up before we're more than two-thirds of the way."

Dunaway trickled smoke as he lifted a gloved hand to point. "I guess some of the cattle didn't stay spooked, did they?"

Alvarado looked out where Dunaway had pointed. There was a fairly large band of the stampeded animals grazing along. They were acting normal, but no stockman would have believed this was so, not after the running panic they had endured. In fact as the riders came closer and the cattle saw them, they flung up their heads, and turned to run again.

Dunaway called to Chalo and that young rider. He gestured for them to turn the cattle, head them southeast. Another man with no burden behind his cantle rode with Chalo and his youthful companion.

Alvarado was scowling. "Southeast ...?"

Dunaway was smashing out his cigarette atop the saddlehorn when he replied. "Yeah. Toward Matanzas."

The burdened men who were riding close around Dunaway and Alvarado watched Chalo and his friends try to turn the cattle. It had turned into a horse race. Alvarado swore and spurred away to lend assistance. Dunaway smiled to himself, and watched as the riders finally got the cattle running in the proper direction. They would run themselves out in a short while because unlike other four-legged creatures, cattle such as those up-graded ones Dunaway was watching had not been bred for speed. They could run for a couple of miles and that was their limit.

One of the riders with Dunaway had trouble with his grisly burden; it continually slipped down the left side of his horse. They had to stop and re-tie the corpse. Otherwise, the ride was uneventful. That pre-daylight cold increased to the point where it would frost garden patches down in town, the men's breath steamed, while elsewhere, toward the east, dawn was on the way.

Dunaway could not make haste because of the horses carrying double. What he had hoped to accomplish was the massacre of all those rustlers, who were the same men who had fired indiscriminately among the buildings back at the ranch-yard killing people in their beds.

It had not turned out that way, nor was he surprised that it hadn't, when he discovered how many rustlers had been driving off the Stuart cattle.

If it had worked, it had been his intention to ride fast down to Matanzas and with another element of surprise, attack Seth Wolf, and to hopefully find him in his bed too.

A long-faced, very dark *vaquero* spoke from directly behind Dunaway. "If we could slip into

Mex-town, they would not know we were among them."

That idea seemed to please the other riders. A man responded in Spanish. "If God wills it, companion. Friends we have down there in Mex-town. They too have reasons for hating Wolf's pirates."

Onix Cepeda shook his head and spoke in English. "It wouldn't work simply because Wolf has informers in Mex-town. Many of them. No; there is no way to make a surprise as we did back yonder."

Dunaway turned toward the prisoner. "You got any ideas?" he asked.

John Rose was glum. "That was what I was goin' to do. Take you fellers over east through the Mex cornfields where you wouldn't look conspicuous, and lead you directly into Mex-town ... I still think it would work, providin' once you got into town you didn't just stand around until someone told Wolf you was there."

Alvarado was waiting on the ground beside his horse when they came along. Dunaway asked how many cattle they were driving. "More than I would have expected," replied the foreman. "Six, maybe seven hundred head, and they're gettin' leg-weary. They're down to a shambling trot. In another mile or so they'll be walking along like they should be."

Dunaway nodded. "Are they being aimed for Matanzas?"

Alvarado had guessed Dunaway's plan, and by

now he had come to like it. "In another two hours the herd will be down there along the north and west sides of town."

Dunaway sent Alvarado back to make certain that was where the cattle would eventually arrive, and caught the dark scowl John Rose had turned in his direction. Dunaway said, "Once, some years back, I was with a big drive, much bigger than what we've got; about six thousand head. We were camping without any stars. It was one of those nights when you can smell rain ... It rained for a fact, but what I remember best is what happened after lightning struck a big old snag-tree directly behind the bed-grounds ... Did any of you ever see a town after six thousand head of blindly stampeding cattle went over it?"

If anyone had seen such a sight, they did not say so now. The old *vaquero* chuckled, and that broke the silence. Several other men also laughed.

Rose had a comment to make. "Matanzas ain't a slab-board town. It's mostly old adobe buildings with walls three feet thick. Ain't no cattle on earth wreck a town that's got three-feet thick walls. All's you're goin' to do, mister, is get a lot of your cattle killed."

Dunaway was watching the brightening new-day world. "John, I never figured we could demolish the town. I just wanted to find a way for us fellers to get in down there without being picked off one at a time if we tried just riding in."

"What was wrong with my idea of sneakin' you in

through the Mex cornfields?"

"Maybe nothing, and then again, maybe you know Wolf has informers in Mex-town."

Six:
Matanzas

Daylight arrived and the cold hung on. By mid-morning they had Matanzas in sight. Dunaway studied the place. He had never seen it before. Nor would he have, in his wildest dreams, expected to arrive down there the way he was shortly to do.

Alvarado drifted back to report that they had picked up more cattle on the south range. Some of these, he said, did not belong to James Stuart.

Dunaway shrugged that off. "How many?"

Carter made a shrewd guess. "Maybe fifteen hundred. Look down there."

It was a sight to warm the heart of any cattleman. The herd was trooping along, perfectly content to be herded toward the clutch of buildings with the old trees lining its one, central roadway.

By now he was sure the herd had been seen. Fifteen hundred head of horned cattle made a wide, deep, and quite long procession. He sent Alvarado to scout the place, and told him to take Chalo Gutierrez with him.

For a full hour they rode in the wake of the big herd with light dust drifting back to settle over them. Alvarado and Chalo were loping past the leaders when two of the herders also cut in front to halt the cattle. They began spreading out in search of feed. Dunaway rose eastward until he saw the wide road which led into Matanzas. When he halted just short of the road John Rose's worried expression deepened. He knew, finally, that Dunaway was not going to back off. He also knew that as Dunaway had told him, if there was a fight, and the outlaw-band down in town saw him among the *vaqueros*, he would indeed have enemies in front as well as in back.

Onix Cepeda was watching Dunaway. The old man had ridden with Mexican route armies, as well as with the *pronunciados* they had been pursuing. Between brigandage and army-sanctioned pillage and murder there was no distinction. Onix had long ago come to believe that the difference between success and failure in any kind of a fight depended upon which side had the best general. He was watching Cab Dunaway with a slight, warm smile. He was certain that this time, he was going to be on the winning side.

The town looked empty. Of course it wasn't, but the arrival of men driving a herd of cattle to its outskirts had sent people scurrying indoors. Under the renegade Seth Wolf, the town's residents had been living with dread and fear for a long time. The sudden appearance of another band of men, driving cattle to the edge of their town, even though it was quite possible this was a legitimate cattle drive, was unusual. Matanzas had no railroad. It did not even have any network of holding corrals for driven herds. People did not know what was happening, they only knew it was very unusual and in their otherwise terrorised situation, it required nothing more to send them into hiding.

But there were others who were not hiding. Dunaway could not see them because he was too distant. Six men were leaning upon an empty tie-rack out front of the Matanzas general store looking up toward the far end of town where two riders were walking their animals in close, while behind those two, other *vaqueros* were keeping the cattle from spreading too much. One of the men dryly said, "Seth and that damned *señorita* of his ... Any of you recognise that light-complected beaner beside the fat-bellied darker one? That's old Stuart's rangeboss or I'll eat my hat."

A lean rider with troubled features squinted, then abruptly left the others hurrying inside the general store. When he emerged with three other men they all turned up the sidewalk and went as far as the last store, then faded back under overhang shade to watch Chalo and Alvarado. One man said, "Somebody better roust Seth out. Maybe he didn't want to be disturbed when we come back from that ambush, but he sure better get his pants on now ... See them other ones farther back?"

Suddenly one of the other men blurted words out. "Jesus! They got dead men behind their saddles." He stepped out of the shade for a better look, then whirled without speaking and went running down the plankwalk. When he reached a narrow dog-trot he ducked down it and eventually came out in Mex-town.

The men he had been up north with turned back as far as the small crowd which was now congregating around the hitch-rack in front of the general store. Among them were survivors of the ambush.

Chalo and Carter Alvarado had seen the sudden activity, so they turned up the roadway toward the place where Dunaway and several of their companions were sitting their horses.

Dunaway was on the ground, hunkering in the shade of his horse, smoking. Close by, as though detailed to act as a bodyguard, Onix Cepeda's black eyes were narrowed as he peered down into the town. It was Onix who identified the pair of loping riders before any of the others could be certain.

Dunaway stamped out his smoke and stood up to greet Alvarado and Gutierrez. Carter spoke as he swung to the ground. "They have been watching us. There is a band of them in front of the general store. One man went running somewhere." He looked steadily at Dunaway. "If we wait much longer they will be ready for us."

Dunaway gazed down into the town. He had never seen the place before in his life and did not know one road from another. He told the men with burdens to take the bodies down and place them beside the road in the shade. Nothing was said until this had been accomplished, then he told Chalo to take several men and bunch the cattle; told him to signal with his hat when he was ready.

After Chalo's departure with several riders, only Carter and Onix Cepeda remained at the roadside with Cabot Dunaway. He turned his attention from the town to the working riders bringing in the wings of the herd. While looking out there he said, "This sure better work ... It's going to be one hell of a mess any way you look at it. They got the cover. All we'll have is cattle and a lot of dust."

Carter grunted, caught Cab's attention and pointed. There was a solitary horseman coming north up the roadway from town. They watched him a long time. Eventually Carter said, "That's the one they call Clampett. The first time Wolf came to the ranch this man came with him. He's a Texan."

Dunaway shed his jacket and tied it behind the cantle. When the man from Matanzas rode up and halted looking down from a wooden face, Dunaway was making his last knot. He glanced around as he said, "Who are you and what do you want?"

Clampett was a thin, rawboned man with close-set dark eyes and a slightly beaked nose. He looked much older than he probably was, wore an ivory-stocked sixgun. "My name is Frank Clampett and I want to know what you think you're ..." Clampett's gaze had found the four dead men lying in a row. He brought his gaze back slowly and made no attempt to speak, to finish what he had started to say. There was a dark stain rising under his cheeks. In Dunaway's view, the man on the horse would become violent with almost no provocation. He had seen men like this before.

John Rose, who had taken a position slightly to the rear of Onix and Carter, eased around them until the mounted man saw him. Clampett's gaze at Rose was flat and uninterested. He turned back toward Dunaway. "Who are you?" he asked softly.

Dunaway ignored the question. "Where is Seth Wolf?"

Clampett did not take his eyes off Dunaway. "You're a damned fool," he said in that same soft tone of voice.

Dunaway strolled around his horse to be fully facing the mounted man. "Get down," he said. Clampett did not move a muscle and neither did he take his eyes off Cab. "Get down, or I'll pull you down, Mister Clampett!"

Finally, Clampett shot a look at Alvarado and Cepeda. He leaned and came to the ground on the left side of his horse. "You better take them cattle away from town," he told Dunaway. "Then you better get on your horse and not even stop for ten days."

Onix flicked his eyes sideways where motion had attracted his attention. A horseman out there was standing in his stirrups flagging with his hat. Onix put his gaze back upon Clampett, but what he said was directed toward Dunaway. "Chalo signalled."

Dunaway acted as though he had not heard. "What did you come out here for?" he asked of the man with the ivory-handled sixgun.

"To find out who you are and what in hell you think you're doing, and to pass the word from Seth Wolf that if you don't turn them cattle, we'll bury you in Matanzas, along with this bunch of beaners you brought along." Clampett looked scornfully from Dunaway to Cepeda and Alvarado, then his gaze stopped upon John Rose. "What are you doin' out here with them, John?"

"I got knocked out last night when they bushwhacked us driving the cattle. They brought me along."

"You better not be with them an hour from now," stated Clampett, and loosened his stance to stand with thumbs hooked in his shellbelt. He turned a little to watch the men bunching the cattle. As he stood watching, Dunaway saw understanding come into his face. As Clampett faced forward again, Cab said, "If it don't work, mister, I'll promise you one thing. You'll sure know you been in a foot race."

Clampett blew out a long breath. "Mister, you're crazy. D'you know that?"

"I'm beginning to suspect it. I've sure heard it often enough lately."

"There are nine of you, as far as I can see. You got any idea how many men work for Seth Wolf?"

"I know he's got five less now than he had yesterday," replied Dunaway, "and with you out of it, that'll be six less. Otherwise, the usual guess is that he has fifteen, not counting himself. That whittles the odds 'way down, Mister Clampett. That makes it man for man."

The outlaw was looking at Dunaway as though he

were a different species. "There are more than nine men down there – not counting me or Mister Wolf?"

Dunaway saw Chalo waving his hat again, and smiled crookedly at Clampett. "Toss your gun down."

Clampett gradually straightened up with all his weight evenly balanced. "Not on your life ... Not even if your friends buy in. You go ahead and try me."

Dunaway met the cruel smile without blinking. "Go ahead and prove it," he said. For several seconds they were completely still, then Clampett's right shoulder hitched, and Dunaway had his own pistol barrel sweeping upwards as the hammer slammed back.

Clampett's weapon cleared its holster but was still pointing toward the ground when he froze, eyes sprung wide.

He was no more astonished than the two men standing beside Cab Dunaway. Alvarado was still staring when Onix Cepeda's leathery, dark face split wide in a grin. He had known all along that this time he was following the right *jefe*.

"Let it drop," Dunaway said.

Clampett obeyed, and Onix stepped in to grab the gun. He stood turning it over and over, cupidity all over his face. He removed his own old weapon from its holster and replaced it with the ivory-gripped weapon, and grinned at Clampett as he held his own old weapon dangling at his side.

Dunaway holstered his Colt and gave Clampett another order. "Turn around."

The outlaw knew all about what was going to happen. He had done it many times, so he did not move. "You'll have to do it with me facin' you, cowboy."

Clampett's colour was a deep, splotchy red. A large vein in the side of his neck was pulsing strongly.

Dunaway started ahead, big work-roughened hands rising as he closed the distance. Clampett knew about this sort of encounter also, and did not wait to be attacked, but rushed Dunaway, bony fists stabbing. He caught Dunaway on the chest and aimed higher as he came in swinging. Dunaway gave ground, twisted to his right, pawed the other man back, then started to move away again, but only in a shuffling way. Clampett rushed in again, swinging hard. Dunaway had not retreated that much. He halted, dug in and smothered a hurting blow over the heart for one chance at Clampett's head.

The blow stopped Clampett flat in his tracks. A streak of claret appeared from his mouth. The vicious expression was gone, in its place was a stunned, dazed look. It was not much of an improvement. Dunaway took two steps and swung from the waist. Clampett went down. Almost before he had stopped moving Onix grabbed him by the ankles and dragged him over to be laid out beside the four dead renegades, then he knelt and very efficiently bound the unconscious man using Clampett's own belts.

Carter Alvarado was watching Cab Dunaway from the side of his eyes. Eventually he said, "I think you broke his jaw."

Dunaway was massaging his right hand and turned toward the horses as he told Onix to truss the other one, the one calling himself John Rose, and leave him over beside the roadway too.

He mounted up, waved his hat back to Chalo, and turned impatiently as Onix made Rose lie on his stomach. Onix worked fast and well. This, too, he seemed to know something about. When he was ready and got astride, Alvarado swung up squinting in the direction of Matanzas.

There were men in the roadway down there. It was impossible to tell whether they had seen what had happened to Frank Clampett, but it was obvious from the number of men down there that Seth Wolf had called out all his riders. It looked to Carter to be perhaps as many as twelve to fifteen men. His heart sank a little. But the distance was too great to make a head-count, and Carter was upset; he was inclined to think things were worse than they actually were – probably because they were.

Chalo and his riders were abandoning the wings and were now congregating along the flank of the cattle. There had been ample time for the cattle to have recovered from their earlier wild run, and none of the riders far back were pushing the herd – not yet – not until it was aimed fully down through the town.

Alvarado did not like being south of the cattle even though they were off to the right of it, near the roadway, so he led off in a big swing which would take them up behind the herd where all the other riders were.

They rode at a lope even though the cattle were just now beginning to be pushed from behind. There was plenty of time, but Alvarado was a worrier and always had been one.

Chalo's wild scream rose over the backs of the moving herd. Other men took it up and finally, someone fired a handgun into the air.

The cattle responded to that, and with pressure from behind, exactly as they had responded to gunfire last night. The leaders broke away in a frantic run directly toward the wide entrance into Matanzas where the stageroad entered town.

Seven:
The Old Vaquero

The ground shook, but excepting the thunder-roll of so many stampeding hooves and the shouts of excited *vaqueros*, there was a silence throughout the town unbroken as the cattle came charging into the upper-end, with some splitting off, being crowded out of the wide roadway, and going down both sides of the thoroughfare, through back-lots, over vegetable gardens, tearing away clothes lines, sending dogs yelping in terror every which way, and knocking over garbage bins, breaking through small wooden fences in a stream of red backs and horns.

The noise finally increased as Wolf's men, who had taken cover among the stores on both sides of the road, began firing weapons. As far as Dunaway could see, as he and the others raced into town through a cloud of thick dust, there was no sign of Seth Wolf's gunmen. The nearest man to him was Onix Cepeda, and at less than twenty feet Dunaway could only intermittently make out his hunched silhouette. But each time the old *vaquero* fired his sixgun Dunaway could see the tongue of flame well enough.

Onix vanished. Dunaway saw a rider on his right swerve for better protection among the buildings, and followed that example. Now, the noise was louder. Cattle pressing close as they raced through town knocked down the posts supporting overhangs. Woodwork came down and disappeared under the hooves and there was more gunfire, even some high-pitched yelling. The glass window in the front wall of the general store shattered into hundreds of pieces. Wooden structures, which were mostly porches and plankwalks, broke into splinters.

Dust nearly as thick as smoke rose in waves. Dunaway left his bay horse in the east-side alley, in someone's buggy-shed, returned to the alley and faced a dozen orry-eyed cattle, slobbering and running with their heads lowered for hooking. He jumped back inside the shed and held his breath when a huge mottled steer struck the building, bounced off and did not even look around. Dust came out of the old rafters and the structure groaned, but it did not collapse.

Dunaway went forward to watch the cattle heading on down the alley, and because the dust was not thick back here where only a dozen or so cattle had charged through, he was able to see a man wearing a flour-sack apron appear in a doorway upon the opposite side of the alley with a shotgun. As the man threw it up to fire into the cattle, Dunaway shot at the doorjamb. The startled man's contorted face swung. Dunaway fired again, lower this time, and the man sprang backwards and slammed his alley door.

Gunfire out along the main thoroughfare was increasing. There were rifles as well as scatterguns, which meant that Wolf's men were pressing the fight. None of the riders who had arrived down here with Dunaway had anything but carbines and sixguns.

There was no order. When Dunaway got up to the main roadway and hung back between two buildings to assess the situation, he could make out a solitary small, ugly building nearly opposite him which had bars over its two small front windows. The door was half open. He had not until this moment thought of the town jailhouse, nor of the lawman who probably had his office over there.

Southward, the cattle had more room as they ran. He watched a roan cow with up-swept long horns hit an upright which supported the roof above the blacksmith shop's outdoors shoeing area. The post snapped, that corner of the roof came part way down, and the roan cow knocked over a forge, an anvil bolted to an oak stump, and sent tools in all directions before she got back into the roadway.

Across from the smithy a man was standing out front of the Matanzas liverybarn frantically waving a white blanket. It was a foolish thing to do; blind-running cattle cannot be spooked off their course. The man flung his blanket at the animals and fled at high speed back down into the roadway. They broke his hitch-rail off at the ground, upset his cedar-log water trough, and one big animal kicked viciously at a wall-bench tearing it loose from the wall.

Opposite Dunaway there was a saddle and harness works with no glass left in its front window. A man moved into the opening swinging a hat at the rolling clouds of dust entering his shop where the window had been. Another man, this one moving stealthily and carrying a carbine up across his body in both hands, came through the harness shop from the rear, roughly shoved the other man aside, and eased up to look both ways along the road, then he suddenly threw up the Winchester. He must have seen someone over on Dunaway's side of the road, but he was aiming northward from Dunaway's dog trot.

Dunaway fired from the hip. Splintering wood showered the rifleman making him recoil as he fired. He jumped back and did not appear again.

Dunaway re-loaded his handgun, caught movement southward and saw Chalo Gutierrez make a wild dash through the dust from the east side of the road to the west side, down beyond the jailhouse. It would have made Dunaway laugh at any other time because Chalo was not built for running. He was straining hard to reach cover among the stores, but his legs simply could not carry him as fast as his spirit wanted them to.

Dunaway searched for someone who might shoot at Chalo but saw no one. He waited until Chalo dove through a broken doorway, then swore at him under his breath. That had been a foolish thing to do.

The cattle were through town and fanning out across open country. Even their noise was diminishing although the great dust-clouds they had scuffed up still floated heavily the full length of the roadway.

The saloon was northward. It had escaped damage, perhaps because it had no wooden awning over the front doorway. Dunaway looked up there, then turned to look southward at the exact moment two men inside the general store opened up on the little building Chalo Gutierrez had disappeared into.

Dunaway crouched and poked his head around to look down there. Smoke from burnt black powder made a soiled-looking mist. Dunaway thought that probably was the store where the man wearing the apron had come out back with a shotgun.

Someone fired back from the little building where Gutierrez had disappeared. All that appeared to accomplish was to enrage the two gunmen inside the store. They fired, levered up and fired again, each man doing this with experienced rapidity. Dunaway waited fruitlessly for one of those riflemen to lean out the shattered window a little. It did not happen. He was twisting to run back to the alley when Chalo fired back with his handgun.

Dunaway reached the alley, looked up and down it, saw a large man with a sixgun in his fist edging around an old rotten wooden fence up near the shed where Cab had tied his bay horse.

The large man was wary. He peered down the alley. Dunaway pulled back from sight, waited, then eased his head out again. The large man eased around the wooden fence with great caution.

Dunaway raised his right hand, waited, and when the large man was clear of the fence hastening toward the shed, Dunaway knocked him down. Instantly, as though his shot had caused it – which it had – a rifleman appeared overhead, upon the roof of the building north of Dunaway's hiding spot. He stared downward into the dusty, lightless runway, and when Dunaway moved, the rifleman saw him.

Dunaway got as close as he dared to the end of the dogtrot. He looked closely in all directions. He did not want to make the mistake the large man had made. For a moment he hung there, then changed his mind about trying to reach the rear door of the general store, and turned back up the runway. That was the movement the man on the roof had detected. With his rifle slanting downward, the man tracked Dunaway, and fired.

The bullet struck time-hardened adobe the span of one hand behind its target. Dunaway jumped ahead and whirled. He did not look upwards until the rifleman on the roof shifted position for a better shot and exposed half his body. He was bending his shoulder around the gunstock and aiming when Dunaway fired. He missed the man but struck the rifle squarely in the wooden forearm beneath the magazine. Under a terrific impact the rifle was hurled upwards. It struck the man in the face. Dunaway saw him fall backwards.

Now, the dust was thinning out. Now too, the fight had settled into a pattern of sniping. Dunaway reached the front dogtrot-opening again just as the gunfire ceased. It was one of those accidental interludes when no one was prepared to fire, and it lasted about two minutes.

Dunaway watched for black powder smoke. There was quite a bit of it down in front of the general store, and to his right, up in front of the saloon. Opposite him and northward, up near where he and his companions had first got into Matanzas, a powerful voice called out.

"You in the *cantina*. I got a surprise for you."

Dunaway braced for the gunfire but it did not come. Evidently whoever was inside the saloon could not place the voice.

Dunaway tried to do that. He probably would have been unable to except that the man with the strong voice called out again.

"Make your peace, *escorio bastardos*!"

Dunaway placed the voice. He also identified it. That had been Onix Cepeda calling out, and he was somewhere in the vicinity of a small, block-like building set apart from any other structure. There were no windows in the ugly little massive building, but the steel-reinforced wooden door hung open.

Someone inside the saloon suddenly cried out. His words were easily distinguishable by the terror which made the man yelling them reach a higher range of sound than probably was his customary tone.

"Get out! Go back to the alley, for Chris' sake – that son of a bitch is in the powder house. *Run*!"

Dunaway threw a startled look in the direction of

the ugly little isolated building, and also hastened back toward the alley. Onix had sounded exultant. How he would manage to blow up the saloon did not concern Dunaway, just the fact that he was in the town's storehouse where dynamite and caps were kept was enough, because if Onix had a way to hurl sticks of blasting powder inside the saloon, and Dunaway was in the dogtrot whose south wall formed one side of the trot, Dunaway would be blown up too.

When he reached the end of his hiding place someone back in the front roadway fired, and this was immediately followed by a furious resumption of the battle. Dunaway crouched and waited, listening as men inside the saloon fought to lift the *tranca* which held the door closed from the inside. He heard someone hurl it aside and the door was flung open. Four men rushed out looking left and right, guns in their hands, but more concerned with fleeing than in being careful.

Dunaway yelled. "Hold it! Stop right there!"

The renegades recoiled from the soil and small stones that bullet had splattered them with, and this time they saw the powder smoke. One man dropped forward and fired. Dunaway shot him through the head. As he was falling another man threw up both arms and yelled that he quit.

Dunaway, with half his head and upper body exposed, waited without breathing until the other two men made a decision. The odds still favoured them, despite one dead companion and another one standing there like a stork with his arms overhead, but the situation did not favour them; they were totally exposed to a man they could scarcely see, and who had demonstrated that he did not miss when he fired.

They dropped their handguns.

Dunaway flagged for them to walk northward up the alley. Short of murdering three unarmed men he had no choice but to step out there too. He went over to them, lined them out and looked over his shoulder. At that moment an ear-splitting explosion made the earth tremble violently. Buildings shook on their foundations. Dunaway's prisoners threw themselves face down. Dirt, stones, and dust rained around them. The sound made Dunaway's ears ring. He was temporarily dazed. Evidently so was everyone else in Matanzas because as the horrendous sound diminished, there was no more gunfire.

Silence settled.

Muted by dust but distinguishable, the triumphant voice of the old *vaquero* came into the sudden hush.

"You see that hole in the road, bastards? That was as far as I could throw. But now I am coming for you. You'd better drink all the whiskey in the saloon. Otherwise it will be blown up with you!"

One of the men on the ground sat up and looked at Dunaway. "Stop him, for Chris'sake."

The other unarmed men also sat up, then they got to their feet beating off dust. There was no fight left in any of them. The frightened outlaws tried imploring Dunaway again. "He's crazy. He'll blow up the whole damned town ... Even if someone shoots the crazy bastard and he's got a lot of dynamite on him ..."

Dunaway considered them. He had no idea what to do with three prisoners. He had no intention of trying to walk across the front roadway with them leading the way to the jailhouse.

Onix called again. He was at the height of his glory. "Wolf? You come out into the roadway. You and the men with you in the store. From where I am now I can throw five sticks through that broken window. *Come out*."

The silence returned, until Chalo Gutierrez yelled in rapid-fire Spanish. Whatever he had said from his hiding place in the small building opposite the general store amused Onix Cepeda. He was laughing when he replied in the same rapid Spanish. Then he switched to English.

"*Señores* in the store, I am crimping the caps ... *Señores*, I will give you a chance to see how good you can shoot ... I am ready to throw them ... But even if you shoot them in the air, they will blow you to pieces ... Are you ready, *Señores*?"

Eight:
Juan-Pedro Althazar

No one answered Cepeda from the store, but neither was there any additional gunfire. It was Chalo calling again in Spanish to his friend that seemed to keep Onix from hurling another stick of dynamite.

Dunaway took his prisoners down to the rear doorway of the store and forced one of them to bang on the door for admittance and call out his name.

No one opened the door and no one called back. Dunaway thought the men inside might have escaped from the building. If so, there was no sign of them in the alley. It did not seem reasonable that they could have fled down the front roadway.

One of his prisoners turned disspiritedly and said, "They're in there, sure as hell. Likely down behind barrels waitin' for the explosion."

Dunaway told the man to kick the door, but the outlaw demurred. Dunaway cocked his Colt. The outlaw went up there, but stood far to one side, and aimed a kick. A door shook, which was what

Dunaway had wanted to know. There was a *tranca* holding it closed. A man might be able to break a lock with bullets but against a thick bar across the inside of the door bullets would have no effect.

The man who had kicked the door called out his name and asked the men inside to allow him to enter. He named the two other outlaws, and he made his plea believable, perhaps because he was not acting.

Still there was no response.

Out front, a man yelled. His outcry was taken up by others, and then Dunaway recognised the voice of Chalo Gutierrez and Carter Alvarado. Moments later he recognised the voice of that young *vaquero*, and Onix Cepeda. There was a rising babble of Spanish, and some tough laughter before one man said in English: "Throw away the guns and lie down on your faces in the road – *pronto*!"

Dunaway motioned for his prisoners to leave the doorway and walk ahead of him southward in the direction of an intersecting side-road. When they got down there, Dunaway turned them to the right and herded them toward the corner of the store building up ahead. He could see over across the road where the liverybarn log trough had poured water over the ground, and where a broken wall-bench was canted half against an adobe wall. There was no sign of human life over there.

Using his prisoners as a shield Dunaway ordered them to move ahead into plain sight upon the east side of the main thoroughfare. They obeyed with reluctance, but nothing happened except that up near the general store several *vaqueros* who were bending over four prone men in the dust craned around with guns rising.

Dunaway called out. The *vaqueros* straightened up from appropriating weapons, watches, finger-rings and silver-mounted spurs. Gutierrez recognised Dunaway behind his prisoners. A broad smile spread across his pock-marked face and white teeth flashed. "*Jefe*," he yelled, "*bueno*! Which one is Wolf?"

They did not have Seth Wolf. They had eight captives, three of whom had been wounded, and there was another dead outlaw inside the general store, plus one behind the saloon in the back alley. Later, they found a badly injured man atop the saloon. They brought him down and took him to a cell at the jailhouse. He had a smashed nose and mouth, and seemed to also have a cracked head.

But although they rounded up local merchants and had them identify the renegades, Seth Wolf seemed to have escaped. One storekeeper told Dunaway that he had seen Wolf go back to Mex-town shortly after that bundle of dynamite had blown the great hole in the roadway.

Dunaway left all but Gutierrez with the captives and passed from the main part of Matanzas down through and out back into Mex-town.

There was not a soul in sight when they got back there. Chalo paused to mop his face and spit cotton, then he pointed to a moderately large adobe structure and led the way. It was a low, massive building opposite the well in the centre of the

Mex-town plaza. Chalo knew the place. Just before they entered he told Cab this was the gathering place for the Matanzas Mexicans. They would smoke in there, drink *cerbeza*, and socialise. Every Mexican town had one place like this which was preferred to all other *cantinas*.

They entered with guns in their hands, and except for sunlight coming through a glassless window in the rear wall, and the front doorway, the large room would have been even gloomier than it was.

Dunaway's eyes made a swift adjustment. Chalo swaggered to the bar on his saddle-warped legs, shoved back his hat and flashed white teeth in a big grin. There were six or eight Mexicans sitting at little tables, as motionless as stone. Some wore guns but the others neither had gunbelts nor looked as though they ever wore them.

Chalo was enjoying himself. He raised his sixgun and pointed it squarely at the face of the thick, perspiring barman, owner of the *cantina*. He asked in Spanish where these people were hiding Seth Wolf and some of his renegades. The fleshy, very dark proprietor spread both hands wide atop his old plank bar and answered quietly. "Mister, we would hide *Satán* before we would hide that murdering rider of other people's horses."

An old man in baggy britches that ended above his ankles and which had once been white, showed toothless gums as he lifted his glass of beer and smiled at Chalo. In Spanish he said, "Rooster! Rest tranquil." Chalo turned slowly aiming his gun at the old man. Instead of cringing the old man drank his beer, bright, bird-like black eyes looking down Chalo's gunbarrel. The old man put down his emptied glass and dragged a soiled sleeve over his toothless mouth, still amused. "I know you," the old man said. "You are a rider for *el patron* Jaime Stuart … If you are going to shoot me …" The old man shrugged thin shoulders then laughed. "Put away the pistol, companion … Put it away and I will tell you something."

Dunaway waited, watching those two. Chalo made his decision slowly and lowered the gun. The old man cackled and Chalo laughed with him. Dunaway let his breath out in a silent long sigh.

"Tell us, then, oldtimer," stated Chalo.

The old man was in no hurry. Dunaway thought he had to be about eighty, but he could have been a hundred. He was as thin and sinewy as they came with a face so wrinkled and weathered it looked like the desert itself. "*Oje*, companion," said the old man, wiping tears of laughter from his eyes. "He took a horse from Candaleria's corral. There was one other wth him. They got another horse from Lopez's shed."

Chalo jerked his head at the proprietor, and two glasses of warm beer were set up. Dunaway did not touch the second glass but Chalo half drained the first one. "Make haste," he told the old man, but it was a waste of breath. The proprietor and his other customers were motionless and expressionless as they regarded the old man.

"I am Juan-Pedro Althazar."

"*Viejo,* as God looks on me I don't care who you are, but unless you stop this game I am going to kill you on your bench." When Chalo finished speaking he lifted out his weapon, and this time he cocked it.

Juan-Pedro Althazar's amusement faded a little and although he reached for the beer glass again, he did not raise it. "It was right after that explosion. Those two came running down here and got those horses ... They were very much afraid. I know. I have seen terror of that kind before. There was a time many years ago when —"

Chalo raised the cocked pistol and aimed it. This time his finger was tightening around the trigger and his black eyes did not have one shred of amusement in them.

The old man gestured. "They rode east. Now it is the interesting thing I will tell you. But first, companion, be aware that I am very poor. I live in rags and go hungry much of the time."

Chalo turned his head in Dunaway's direction. "The old bastard wants money," he said in English.

Dunaway fished in a pocket and flung some sweat-damp, crumpled greenbacks at the old man's feet. Chalo turned back, still with the cocked gun aimed. "What is interesting, old one? I am going to blow your head apart!"

The old man bent with an effort, retrieved the money and said, "You can overtake them, gentlemen. Candaleria's horse has no shoes and is very tender-footed. Lopez's horse is crazy. *Loco*. All you must do is find their tracks. A child could do it. Candaleria was going to shoe his horse today, so he pared the hooves down even more." The old man pocketed the money and smiled until his wet gums were exposed. "That horse cannot travel five miles, and the one they took from Lopez's shed has been in one place standing eating lupin." The old man laughed.

Several of the other patrons of the saloon smiled, but others, including the sweating, fat saloonkeeper, did not laugh. They relaxed a little though, as Chalo eased down the hammer of his weapon and put the gun in its holster while he regarded Juan-Pedro Althazar. He turned to range a look among the other Mexicans, settled on a younger, stalwart man and said, "He is probably lying to get some money, eh?"

The rather handsome stalwart man shook his head looking directly at Chalo Gutierrez. "No, mister … I am Epifanio Lopez."

"It was your crazy horse, then, friend?"

"Yes. He may be ridden a mile, two or three miles, until he goes crazy. Then there is no buckaroo alive who can stay on his back."

"Why would you keep a crazy horse, friend?"

The younger Mexican looked troubled. "I raised him, mister. He was orphan with good blood." The man shrugged.

Chalo dug deep and dropped several large silver coins atop the bar. "Give them more beer," he told the saloonman, and turned toward the door.

Back outside where visibility was much better, he explained what had been said to Cab Dunaway, then he grinned while wiping off sweat. "Where is your bay horse?"

Dunaway pointed toward the alley. "Get yours and meet me over here as fast as you can."

"What about the others?"

"They don't need us. Get your horse."

As they parted Chalo looked back with a big smile. "That was good beer, you should have tried it."

What Dunaway wanted was cold water, and he got it after leading his horse out of the ramshackle shed. There was a little *acequia* behind an old wooden fence which irrigated someone's rows of maize and beans. He and the horse both tanked up, then he got astride and turned northward toward the upper end of town.

The wait was short. Chalo came loping up with his hat pulled down to keep sunsmash from his eyes. They loped eastward until they were beyond Mex-town, then they split up and quartered.

Horse-sign was everywhere, but when Dunaway saw two sets of barefoot marks, he whistled, flagged with his hand, and Chalo hastened to catch up.

The air above Matanzas was dust-tan even yet. Otherwise the country they rode over had glass-pure visibility. Dunaway could see no riders up ahead, and privately wondered about the old Mexican's veracity. But they had not covered enough ground yet to be certain one way or another, and they had fresh barefoot hoof-tracks to follow, which convinced Chalo Gutierrez they would overtake the fleeing renegades, if his riding partner had doubts.

Dunaway swept down a long slope and went up the far side with Chalo a few yards to the rear. Atop the rise Dunaway hauled back and pointed.

The ground was torn and scarred where a horse had bucked. It had been quite a battle. The horse had fought like a demon over an area of not less than two acres. But there was no man on foot in sight. Chalo pursed his lips in an admiring whistle. "He is one hell of a rider, *jefe*, whoever he is."

There was no question about that. As Dunaway resumed the trail and studied the distance, he speculated upon the man who had battled the loco horse to a standstill. If the man was as good with weapons as he was at bucking out crazy horses …

Chalo was standing in his stirrups, pointing.

Southward a dozen degrees down where there was a bosque of straggly trees, two riders emerged from the shadows heading due south. They had not seen Cab nor Chalo, but before long it was inevitable that they would see them, because there was not enough sheltering undergrowth to the south to prevent this.

Chalo laughed. "We can worry them to death," he told Dunaway. "We can walk them down. Do you see the big horse out front?"

Dunaway had been watching the leading horse. Even at that distance it was obvious that the tall horse was mincing. If they had not known better, they might have thought he was sore in the shoulders, but they knew better – he was walking on eggs. Every tiny sharp bit of rock he stepped on made a stone bruise. Eventually he would be unable to even stand in one place without favouring.

The second horse was acting the way some locoed horses behaved. He was walking directly behind the tall horse with his nose within inches of the lead-horse's tail. If a horse was loco enough he could not even be led. Nor would he drink water nor eat. But clearly this crazy horse was not that far advanced, otherwise the renegade on his back would never have been able to ride him out of Mex-town.

However, it might have been better for the renegade on his back if he had been that loco. It would have been obvious and the renegade would have searched out and stolen another animal.

Chalo was happy. Dunaway rolled and lit a smoke, watched the fleeing men, and finally matched Chalo's smile. Shortly now the fleeing men would see them. They had two choices; to try and out-run the pursuit, which they would not be able to do, or they could find a place suitable for protection, fort-up and fight.

There was a third alternative, but as Dunaway rode along smoking, he was almost positive the renegades would not do it. They could stop, throw down their weapons and raise their hands.

If they were taken back to Matanzas the people would hang them as surely as God had made little green apples.

Nine:
The Black Rock Place

Dunaway knew the exact moment the outlaws saw their pursuers. The rider in front on the tall horse half reined around and his gimpy mount flinched.

Chalo, who did not smoke, mopped off sweat and rode along studying the onward country. There were several places men might fort-up, but none of them looked particularly secure, so, wherever they made their stand, since out-running the pursuit was out of the question, the renegades had no choice but to fort-up in a place they had been driven to from desperation. That pleased Chalo.

It was a bizarre chase. Neither the renegades nor their pursuers rode out of a walk for a long while. And they gained steadily.

Dunaway glanced back. Dust was still visible over Matanzas, but it was fading. Otherwise, there was no rider coming from that direction. He preferred for the men under Carter Alvarado to clean up the town.

He straightened forward as Chalo spoke. "That is

Wolf on the tall horse. You see? He is a tall, strong man. When you are closer you will see that he has a mean face too ... The other one, I don't recognise, but none of us have been to Matanzas in a long while. He could be someone Wolf brought in ... He sits a horse like an Indian."

Dunaway let these observations pass. He was watching the tall horse begin to limp in the direction of some scaly black rocks which had a few pines growing among them. The rocks were not high enough to protect a man, unless he got down upon one knee, and the trees were too irregularly spaced to help much.

But there was no other place to fort-up anywhere in sight, although southward a fair distance there was more broken country as well as more scrub timber.

Dunaway said, "We got 'em, Chalo."

Gutierrez did not answer. His eyes were puckered nearly closed. He watched the renegades aim for that rocky place, and spat in scorn. All those rocks would do for Wolf and his partner was prolong the killing.

They halted out of Winchester range and dismounted to stand in horse-shade watching the outlaws get in among the rocks. They tied their horses to tree limbs, took saddleguns and went forward to face Chalo and Cab Dunaway. It had seemed to Dunaway that the renegades moved slowly, tiredly. Or maybe disspiritedly, since they would realise their battle-ground was not good enough.

Chalo wagged his head. "Fools. Well, one of us can go around behind. One of us can stay in front."

Dunaway was silent. There was sheltering underbrush for the attackers to within ten yards of the rocks. True, underbrush would not deflect bullets, but on the other hand if he and Chalo were careful, they could get within shooting range without being seen. He turned. "Partner, they'll want our horses more than our scalps."

Chalo agreed. "I will ride around and get behind them," he said. "If I can get close enough to fire near the loco horse, he will come apart. Then they will have only one horse."

Dunaway said, "Be damned careful. They got damned little to lose."

Gutierrez was turning to swing back up over leather, when he smiled back at Dunaway. "*Jefe, en el pais de las ciegos, el tuerto es rey.*" At Dunaway's expression, Chalo laughed. "It means that in the land of the blind, the one-eyed is king." He gestured toward the rocks from his saddle. "We are kings here. There is no need to take chances. If we cared to we could just sit down and let thirst do it for us."

Chalo rode away, making a very wide half-circle. He could not see the renegades but they could see him, most of the time, and it required no great brilliance to guess what he was doing – riding around so as to be able to shoot at them from the rear.

Dunaway rolled and lit another cigarette. He saw a man shift position among the ugly old black rocks, and guessed he was seeking a fresh shelter so as to be able to protect their rear. Dunaway tossed down his smoke and called out.

"Wolf! It's useless. You're on foot. There'll be a small army out here directly."

The reply was a carbine shot which did not quite reach Dunaway. Dunaway spat, watched Gutierrez far to the west begin walking his horse down behind the rocks. Dunaway led his horse back into a heavy stand of buckbrush and left him tethered there, took his saddlegun and went back, but closer this time, working his way back and forth through the underbrush. There was a wide strip of open country between the brush and the rocks, but Dunaway did not have to cross it. He was already well within Winchester range when he settled on one knee with a huge old thornpin bush in front. He eased springy limbs aside and peered out.

There was no sign of either renegade. They would be belly-down behind the rocks now. He searched the west country for sign of Gutierrez, and saw him finally. He was walking his horse steadily in the direction of the rocks. Dunaway watched, hoping very hard Chalo could gauge the distance. If he got too close he was going to be shot at.

Chalo halted, dismounted with a carbine in his hand, and squatted down in front of his horse like an Indian. He moved twice, both times to his right, which was southward. He was either trying to get into a better position for shooting, or he was deliberately forcing the renegades to watch him instead of Dunaway.

There was a strong scent of greasewood and creosote bush in the still air. Lizards scurried from bush to bush in search of insects. They paid no more attention to Dunaway than they did to the little black rocks with which the ground out here was sprinkled.

Dunaway raised his carbine, took a long rest on a large thornpin limb, and squeezed off a shot. The bullet flew true and exploded off a rock, scattering lead fragments and bits of sharp rock.

He waited for the return fire. There was none. He shifted position and fired again, this time trying to hold true on the lip of a rock. The bullet broke away a large segment of the prehistoric, old brittle stone, along with a flurry of smaller scraps, and this time he saw a gunbarrel come around into a stone slot, and dropped flat.

The renegade's shot was into the bush on Dunaway's left, close enough to inspire respect for the shooter, but not close enough to do anything else. Dunaway fired directly at the exposed gun barrel, struck rocks inches from it, and rolled.

This time when the gunfire erupted it was from a different position. Dunaway pushed off sweat with a sleeve and did not answer that shot. He knew where they were lying.

From the west a solitary carbine shot sounded spitefully out where Chalo was hiding behind a big bush. The renegades did not face around or fire back, which meant that Chalo's bullet had not come close to them.

A bull-bass voice suddenly called ahead. "You

can't get us, not if you use up all your ammunition."

Chalo fired again, an angling shot from the northward underbrush. There was more brush over where he was, almost a wall of it.

Through the echo of gunfire Dunaway called back. "Wolf, if you wait until the hang-mob gets out here ..."

There was no reply. Dunaway squirmed into a fresh position and this time, with his carbine lying atop a circular, flat black stone, he waited for a target. He did not have enough loads left to keep up this duelling.

Chalo made an exultant scream, the way Indians did. Dunaway was certain both the renegades would roll over and look back. It would have been an ideal time to go after them, except that he could no longer be certain where they were. He swore, hitched his carbine a few degrees northward, and lay there waiting.

Someone among the rocks fired in the direction of Chalo's scream. Dunaway knew he would no longer be at that spot, and pulled a few Winchester cartridges from his shell-belt, methodically shoved them into the Winchester, then got back down again to rest his weapon atop the same flat, round rock.

Silence settled. That bothered Dunaway more than the shooting. He had never in his life underestimated an enemy, and did not do it now. He shifted position again, moving northward with a flight of stinging deer-flies following him.

The silence endured. Dunaway brushed at the flies and found another good position. He was completely hidden from the men in the rocks.

Suddenly, Chalo opened up, firing three times so fast it sounded almost like one prolonged gunblast. No one fired back. Dunaway was sweating like a stud horse. Wolf was up to something. Any man as bold and resourceful as Seth Wolf was, would have known some time ago that he was on the losing side in this kind of a fight.

It came to a head suddenly and swiftly. The crazy horse had been fighting his tie-shank and finally broke loose. He ran belly-down directly toward the rocks where Wolf and his companion were lying. Two handguns blew the silence apart in an almost simultaneous blast of gunfire. The loco horse went up into the air and came down rolling end over end. Dust flew and a man screamed.

Dunaway recklessly arose to one knee and pushed branches aside. He could see the dead horse lying sideways up near the front of one of the big black rocks. He also saw a man struggling frantically to roll the inert thousand-pound animal. Before Dunaway could lift his carbine, Chalo fired from much closer out through the underbrush. The straining man's tense muscles turned loose like coiled springs. He went straight up to his full height, seemed to be reaching for something in the air, then he collapsed across the dead horse.

Now, the silence that arrived was worse than before. There was a dead renegade over in the rocks, which Chalo could not see but who was in

Dunaway's sight. Dunaway's guess, from that scream, was that the shot horse's furious momentum had carried him right up where the outlaws had been, and he had fallen atop one of them. That scream had had a sound of pure fright in it.

Dunaway looked over where a small cloud of dirty gunsmoke hung near the bush where Chalo had been when he had fired. Of course Chalo would no longer be there but Dunaway yelled to him anyway.

"Can you see them, Chalo?"

The answer arrived from many yards southward. "I see the horse. Where is the one I fired at?"

"Dead. He's on my side of the horse. Where is the other one?"

Before Chalo could reply an unsteady voice rose in gasps. "It's over ... Get this horse off me."

Dunaway stood up and still could not see enough of the dead animal to be sure there was indeed a man pinned over there. "Wolf?" he called. "Throw out your guns."

The breathless voice answered instantly. "I can't. I can't get my arms free. Get him off me! I quit. Just get this damned horse off me."

Dunaway saw Chalo suddenly appear out of the underbrush. The pinned man could not see him because he could not see over the horse. Dunaway yelled to Gutierrez. "Be careful. Don't trust 'em."

Chalo started walking, handgun in his right fist. He was trailing his carbine. He reached the edge of the field of black rocks, halted to methodically lean aside his Winchester, then walked forward again.

He stopped abruptly and hurled his thick body sideways. One second later a gunshot erupted. Dunaway's anger came up in red waves. He started around the underbrush, Winchester in both hands and cocked. He ran across the open area without even thinking. When he came up to the first of the big rocks, he raised the carbine. From the corner of his eye he could see Chalo frantically crawling for cover, and a man sitting up with a dead horse across his lower legs was tracking Gutierrez.

Dunaway squeezed the trigger. The pinned outlaw's gun went off from a muscle spasm. The bullet barely cleared the dead horse and fractured a large boulder. Then the renegade turned loose all over and dropped back.

Dunaway levered up and went closer. The first man had been hit squarely through the middle of his chest. Whether Chalo was that good a marksman, or it had been an accident, the result was the same. That renegade had been dead before he had dropped across the horse.

The second man was hatless. He had a vicious cast to his features, greying hair, and a small puckered bluish hole in his right temple.

Chalo was sitting up looking at his torn shirt where blood was running. When Dunaway walked over and extended a hand, the Mexican allowed himself to be pulled to his feet. He fished for an old bandana and mopped at the blood. Then he glanced up and said, "They got a canteen?"

Dunaway leaned on his carbine eyeing Gutierrez.

"How bad is it?"

Chalo looked down then up. "This? He didn't hit me. These rocks are as sharp as razors. Are they both dead?"

"Yes."

"Then I want to see if they had a canteen." Chalo walked over and stood gazing downward for a long while, then he shook his head. "No canteen," and twisted to look for the tall horse. He went bandy-legging it out to that animal, but it did not have a canteen on the saddle either.

When he returned it required all the strength of them both to roll the horse off the dead outlaw. Chalo sat down upon the horse and gazed at the corpses. "Which is Wolf?" he enquired.

Dunaway made a safe guess. "The one the horse fell on. Nobody said Wolf was a 'breed', and this other one is at least half Indian."

Chalo raised his sweat-shiny, dirty face. "Riders from Matanzas. Maybe one of them'll have a canteen. I been spitting cotton for two hours."

For Cab Dunaway the killing of Seth Wolf was the ending. He was wrong, but since he did not know this, he put his back to the corpses and watched the mob of horsemen loping toward him from the direction of Matanzas. Whether they had a canteen or not, they could at least pack the dead renegades back to town.

Ten:
Toward Sundown

There was enormous relief in the town. Undoubtedly there was also happiness because the community had been delivered from murdering renegades, but there was no atmosphere of elation when the riders turned up the main thoroughfare, silently dismounted and carried the pair of dead renegades over in front of the jailhouse where two of their dead companions had been propped up, backs to the jailhouse wall, legs and feet straight out across the plankwalk. Chalo was turning away when a stalwart Mexican brushed his sleeve and asked in Spanish what had been the fate of the loco horse.

Chalo told him, also speaking Spanish, and when the stalwart man's face fell, Chalo patted him on the back, saying that if it had not been for the loco horse, the outlaws might have escaped, which was not quite the truth but that did not matter. The owner of the dead horse shuffled away saddened by the loss of his animal, but also consoled, and Chalo gazed after him wondering why anyone would want to keep a crazy horse. He shrugged and went in search of some cold water.

Onix Cepeda, smiling broadly and with six waxed red dynamite cylinders stuck into his shellbelt, told Dunaway several of the town merchants were up at the saloon and wanted to see him. Dunaway allowed a big-eyed youth to lead his horse down to the liverybarn, and entered the jailhouse, which smelled powerfully of carbolic acid. A woman from Mex-town who was by reputation a healer had been to see the wounded man with the shattered face. When Dunaway passed his open cell door and glanced in, there was nothing showing but the man's eyes, and they did not focus. Carter Alvarado eased up shaking his head. "He will probably die. His skull is broken."

Three of the downcast Texans in an adjoining cell had also been bandaged. The uninjured men were in an opposite cell. They too sat gazing out at Dunaway and the men who had entered the cell-room with him. Only one of them had even a hint of defiance in his face. The others looked beaten.

Dunaway turned to the men behind him and asked where John Rose was, the renegade they had captured out where the stolen cattle were being driven. Eyes went from face to face. Alvarado spread his hands. "I don't know."

No one knew. The last any of them had seen of the prisoner had been about the time the battle started in town. Onix said, "Why does it matter?"

Dunaway regarded the old rogue. It probably did

not matter. One thing was reasonably certain, John Rose would never return.

People were crowding into the small jailhouse office, and one of them pushed, elbowed, growled and shoved through until he was facing Dunaway. He smiled, exposing toothless gums. He spoke in Spanish. "Chief, remember it was Juan-Pedro Althazar who made it possible for you to conquer these pirates."

Chalo Gutierrez was shouldering through and halted directly behind the old man. Without a word he reached from behind, enclosed Juan-Pedro Althazar in powerful arms, lifted the old man off his feet, and turned, with the old man struggling, calling down curses on everyone, and trying to kick Chalo in the chins while he was carried out to the plankwalk and put down.

He whirled on Chalo, old eyes blazing. He called him a number of select names and aimed a kick which Chalo blocked. In the roadway someone laughed. It was taken up by men in the jailhouse doorway. Chalo reddened, scooped up a fistful of the furious old man's cotton blouse, pulled him in so close their noses almost touched, then Chalo spat a savage sentence at him in Spanish, released the old man and gave him a shove.

Juan-Pedro Althazar scuttled in a towering rage across the roadway and disappeared down through one of the dogtrots which led back to Mex-town.

Gradually, the plankwalks filled with townpeople. Onix was at the height of his glory. That younger *vaquero* who had been so anxious to be in the fight was much less conspicuous. It had indeed been a furious fight, but the sight of those four bloody corpses propped out front of the jailhouse for everyone to view made him grow up fast.

A slightly stooped, tall, greying man with a white face and tapered long white fingers came up to Dunaway at the jailhouse hitchrack, and offered a pale hand. His name was Clarence Black, he owned the general store. Dunaway leaned on the tie-rack gazing at him, and when the words of profuse gratitude began to pour out, Dunaway cut in to say, "Something I wondered about, Mister Black: What happened to your town lawman?"

Black swallowed. "He left the same day those others rode in."

"How many folks live in Matanzas?"

"Well; by the last count about four hundred."

"How many of them were men?"

Finally, the tall, stooped man saw where this discussion was leading, and got pink in the face. "We're not gunfighters, Mister Dunaway. We're peaceable folks. We couldn't go up against that many killers. No one could expect us to."

"Maybe not," agreed Dunaway, conscious of the crowd standing around listening. "But I'm not a gunfighter and neither are any of these Stuart ranch *vaqueros* who came down here with me. And we didn't number ten men."

The tall man protested. "We wouldn't have had a chance. They killed people. Shot them out of hand. We have families to think of, and businesses."

Dunaway pushed up off the tie-rack and pressed

through the crowd without another word. Back at the tie-rack men were gazing at the ruined woodwork where the cattle had broken everything they struck. Others were gazing at the dust. Mister Black the storekeeper stared at Dunaway's retreating figure, red to his hairline, then he turned and marched stiffly over to his store, where the glassless front window gaped, and disappeared inside.

It required all the persuasive powers of Carter Alvarado and Chalo Gutierrez to dissuade Onix from going down to Mex-town with his belt full of those dynamite sticks. In the end they prevailed, and as they went southward in search of their saddlestock the other Stuart ranch riders joined them, leaving the town-people to gaze upon the wreckage, which included a large hole in the middle of their roadway, up in front of the saloon.

It was easier to go in search of their saddle animals than it was to actually locate them. Dunaway waited in front of the liverybarn. When they were all mounted he led them south down below town where the cattle were spreading east and west as they cropped off short grass.

They did not complete the gather until late. As they began pushing the gather northward, well over on the west side of town, a top buggy with yellow running gear came across country at a spanking rate and caught up with the riders about two miles northward. Alvarado rode over with Cab Dunaway and when they were fairly close, Carter leaned and said, "That's the mayor. He owns the saddle and harness works."

The mayor was a bull-necked older man with work roughened hands, several prominent gold teeth, a ruddy complexion and a shrewd smile. As he alighted to introduce himself to Dunaway he said, "We was waitin' at the saloon. Guess you didn't hear that we wanted to see you."

Dunaway swung off, pumped the mayor's hand, then stood waiting. He was tired to the bone. He had not enjoyed anything he'd had to do this day.

The mayor brought a formal pronouncement of gratitude to Dunaway and his riders from the residents of Matanzas. Dunaway watched the drag pass, with two riders keeping it moving. When the mayor had said his piece Dunaway smiled and nodded. "I'm obliged. The men who came down here with me did more than I did. And we didn't do it so much to save your town, Mister Mayor, as we did it to pay someone back for killing James Stuart and trying to steal his cattle. But we appreciate what you said."

The mayor's genial face smoothed out. "James Stuart is dead?"

"Yeah. Him and some of his people, including a pregnant woman and a little kid. Mister Mayor, if you were to hang those prisoners I wouldn't feel bad at all."

The mayor remembered something. "We had a meeting of the Town Council. Someone said those men have bounty money on them. By unanimous vote of the Council we're in favour of you collecting it ... James Stuart is dead?"

Dunaway was turning to mount his animal.

"Yeah, dead." He swung up, nodded and loped after the drovers.

The mayor stood a while gazing northward, then climbed into his little rig and turned back toward town. He had known James Stuart since he'd arrived in the Matanzas countryside, and that had been a long time ago. He had known Stuart's wife and daughter. It was bad enough to have his town taken over by renegades, then nearly destroyed by the men who had put an end to the outlaw reign, but losing an old friend was much harder. As he wheeled back into town he left his rig at the liverybarn and walked northward to the telegraph office which was on the same side of the road as his harness works.

The day had taken a toll of them all. Tequila would have helped but they did not have any. Even whiskey, of which the *vaqueros* were not particularly fond, would have helped. All they had was some tobacco, and not all of them smoked.

They pushed the cattle hoping to get them back on their own range before nightfall. They made it, but mainly because the cattle were as eager to get back as the men were to get them back.

They rode the rest of the way under a fading sky with little to say, until Alvarado looked around and announced what the others already knew: They had not suffered a single casualty, unless they counted Chalo's torn shirt and multiple stone-scratches. One of the men said it was because the Good Lord had watched over them. No one took this up, elaborated on it or contradicted it.

When they entered the yard people came running from the little houses. They'd had a long day of dread, fear and uncertainty. All of it dissolved when they saw that every man who had ridden out had also ridden back. Wives clung to sweaty *vaqueros*, children ran among the horses. Dunaway led his animal into the barn to be off-saddled, and nearly fell over a man lying on the ground bound and gagged, and trying hard to get out of the way of the horses.

The other men who had also brought their horses inside stopped with equal astonishment, and stared. A heavy-set, very dark woman came in with Chalo Gutierrez and pointed as she rattled off some Spanish.

Chalo disengaged his arm, went up and leaned over the stranger fighting his bonds. "Hey, *amigo*," he said, "you were supposed to be here four days ago."

Dunaway stood frowning. "Who is he, Chalo?"

"His name is Baxter, *jefe*. He is the man *el patron* sent for. He it is who was supposed to come along when we found you."

"Turn him loose. Who tied him up, anyway?"

Chalo rolled his eyes in the direction of the hefty woman. She was Chalo's wife. Dunaway turned, the woman ignored him to watch her husband free the gunfighter. He asked her why she had tied the stranger.

The woman raised her eyes, finally. "He rode in drunk and making a lot of noise. We were mourning. I told him to leave and he laughed at me.

So when he climbed down all the other women came over to help. We threw him down, took away his guns, and – that is how we left him."

As Dunaway turned to face the angry gunman, he saw smiles spreading among the tired *vaqueros*. He and Baxter faced each other. Dunaway held out his hand, palm upwards. "How much of Mister Stuart's money do you have left?"

The gunfighter glared at Dunaway while rubbing his wrists. "Who are you?" he snarled. "And what business is it of yours?"

While Dunaway was beginning to answer, someone cocked a sixgun behind Baxter, and silence came very suddenly. Baxter went white in the face. Dunaway nodded toward his upturned hand. "The money."

Half of it had not been spent. Baxter handed it over, then turned slowly to see the broadly smiling face of Onix Cepeda above the cocked sixgun. He turned back toward Dunaway. "Where is Mister Stuart?" he asked.

"Dead. If you hadn't been drunk and bothersome they'd have told you. Where is your horse?"

Baxter did not know but Chalo's wife jutted her chin in the direction of the corrals out back. Dunaway said, "Get on him, and don't come back."

They all stood silently watching the gunfighter stamp out of the barn. Dunaway turned to face Chalo's wife again. He winked at her and smiled.

Eleven:
Blood!

There were things Dunaway suspected, but never having been on an historic Spanish cattle ranch before, he did not quite understand. Where he came from cowmen hired riders for the season and paid them off when it was over. Here, the *vaqueros* lived on the ranch with their wives and children, some had been born here. It was a closely-knit, isolated and private community, each with the interests of the others at heart. While he was sleeping away the night, and on into the newday sunshine of the following morning, the residents of Stuart ranch were busy with other things.

The women laid out *el patron*, bathed him, put fresh clothing on him, wailing as they did these things, and Chalo's hefty wife entwined a rosary around his hands where they lay at rest upon his chest.

They did the same for the other dead victims of the murderous attack by Seth Wolf's renegades. Someone even made a comfortable little burial pallet for the small dog which had been killed.

Like all the old Spanish ranches, there was a cemetery which had been sheltering the ranch-dead for more than half a century. It was a half-mile northward upon a flat rise of grassland where trees grew.

It was the slow *careta* procession heading out there that awakened Cab Dunaway, but by the time he had scrubbed, shaved and dressed, the dolorous mourners were almost to the trees.

He stood in front of the barn soberly watching; thinking it was better that he had not been included. He was a stranger, an outsider, not entirely because he had only ridden in a couple of days earlier, but because none of the customs or traditions of these people were his.

He faced around at the soft summons of a woman. In the doorway of a *jacal* she stood looking across the yard at him. When he faced her she said something in liquid Spanish, of which he understood one word, 'breakfast'.

He crossed over to the house. She had lacings of grey over both ears, otherwise her hair was midnight-black and had been brushed until it shone. She was a handsome fifty years, her body kept strong and supple by labour. When he removed his hat she turned without a word and led him inside where the smell of many meals layered the shadowy interior.

A rough wooden table with benches stood near an adobe oven which had been built into a corner of one wall. There was food on the table. When the woman saw him hesitate, she told him in Spanish to be seated.

She brought black coffee and hot *salsa* for his eggs. They had been cooked with *chorizzo* and while they were actually mild by southwestern standards, Dunaway thought they were very spicy. He asked the woman if she understood English. She smiled; it peeled thirty years from her. "Yes. But we don't speak it often. There is no reason."

He asked about the funeral procession and she explained how it was, on the old ranches. She explained a number of things and when Dunaway asked why she had remained behind, she said very simply because it was the obligation of someone to be here when *el jefe* – the chief – was ready to be fed.

She told him he was a hero, and when the other rancheros who had suffered at the hands of Seth Wolf and his Texans heard what had happened, who had thought up the strategy and had led the *vaqueros*, they would come over to see this formidable *yanqui*, and to offer their friendship and gratitude.

Dunaway finished eating, pushed aside the plate and pulled in the cup of coffee. In Spanish he said, "Your name is what?"

She was the wife of Carter Alvarado. Every woman on the ranch was the wife of someone. She was also the half-sister of the wife of Chalo Gutierrez, had been born on the ranch, and was related to several of the other retainers. At Dunaway's quizzical expression she asked if he found all of this strange.

He did, and told her why; that where he came from married riders were rarely hired, and when they were, it was almost unheard-of for their wives to be allowed to live on the ranch.

The handsome woman thought about that as she came forward to refill the coffee cup. When their eyes met she said, "Like the Indians; a woman is fit only to load the pack animals, gather wood and make meals, eh? We are more civilised, *jefe*." She watched his face. "You have never been in this country before?"

"No."

The liquid dark eyes remained on his face. "Do you like it, *jefe*?"

He considered the coffee she had poured. "I rode south from Raton, through Durham, and met your husband and his friends a couple of days ago. Until then I had never seen any of you, or this ranch – or Matanzas."

The woman understood. "You saw the worst part, *jefe*, but it must be the same everywhere."

He nodded and arose after finishing the coffee. He smiled at her and drew again upon his limited Spanish. "*Gracias, Señora.*"

She smiled back. "*Por nada, jefe* ... They will be back soon."

He wandered over to the barn to make certain his bay horse had been cared for. It had, so he strolled around front and leaned on the hitchrack where springtime sunshine, without wind, was mantling this world of old customs with a soft shade of gold.

He could see the people northward upon that flat landswell among the trees, and thought about the frail, gentle man they were burying among his retainers. He made a smoke and also thought of his old friend Sam Cutler. He had never killed a man in quite the way he had shot Seth Wolf yesterday. It had been more nearly an execution than a shoot-out. He had no regrets at all.

With Sam dead there was no reason for him to linger. The working season would be fully underway by the time he could get back up north, but a tophand could get a job.

If he couldn't, if all the big outfits had already hired their full working crews, then he would perhaps go into the mountains, find a blue-water lake, of which Colorado and Wyoming had hundreds, set up a camp and loaf. He had earned the right.

The procession was returning, most of the people walking with their heads lowered. As Dunaway watched, he thought it might be best if he was gone before they reached the yard. He was an outsider. This was their period of grief and he would not fit into it.

As he turned to enter the barn a flat voice speaking softly gave him an order. "You son of a bitch, I'm going to kill you! Keep your hands out front ... Now then, where is that money you took off me last night?"

He knew approximately where the gunfighter was, but without movement to help, and with the perpetual gloom inside the old barn to hinder his effort to locate Frank Baxter, he would only get himself killed if he made a fight of it. "I gave the money to the foreman to keep until Mister Stuart's heirs show up."

"Where did he put it?"

Dunaway honestly had no idea. But he knew better than to suggest that Alvarado might have hidden it in the *jacal* across the yard. Baxter would kill the handsome woman too. "I got no idea what he did with the money ... Did you see them coming back from up yonder where they buried their dead?"

Baxter did not reply, but he stepped out of the darkness behind the harness-pole to face Dunaway. His face was beard-stubbled and deadly.

"Ask him," Dunaway told the gunfighter.

Baxter remained silent. He seemed to believe what Dunaway had said, and he also seemed to be struggling to find a way to resolve the predicament. Cold frustration made him say, "I'll kill you anyway."

Dunaway was standing like a statue with both arms in front. "You shoot that gun, and you'll have them boiling around here like hornets."

Evidently this was what Baxter had been thinking. "I'm goin' to get that money. Stuart sent it to me and it was mine. If I have to fight the whole bunch of them I will."

"Big odds," exclaimed Dunaway. "You'll be taking a hell of a risk for a hundred or so dollars."

This too, the gunfighter knew. But it was not altogether the money; it was the need of a swaggering gunman to erase the humiliation he had suffered when those women had borne him to the ground and had tied him, then had dragged him into the barn to lie like a shoat awaiting slaughter.

Nothing like that had ever happened to Frank Baxter before.

Dunaway guessed about half of this. He had known gunmen before. They were all different except in one way, they could not live with humiliation. "You had a good time with the money he sent you, and which you spent. You could leave it at that."

Baxter sneered, said nothing, and walked around Dunaway to the barn opening and peered northward.

Dunaway, with his back to the gunfighter, guessed about what Baxter was doing, and assessed his chances, but Baxter had turned back by the time Cab had reached a decision. In the same bleak tone of voice the gunman said, "You're the big hero ... They wouldn't shoot their hero, would they? If I was behind him and they was in front ... They'd hand over the money."

Dunaway's reply to that was rueful. "Baxter, there are eight men. Sure, they'll likely hand over the money – and any other money they can scrape up ... Now just tell me: How do you get away afterwards? This is their country. They can read sign as good as an Indian. And there are eight of them to run you down ... Baxter, forget it."

The gunfighter cursed, looked one last time out where the slow-moving procession was nearing the yard in sunlight, then he walked down in front of Dunaway and stood glaring. "I figured you'd have kept it."

"Search me. I told you the truth. It wasn't my

money. I gave it to the foreman. Turn my pockets inside out if you like. I don't have a red penny of that money."

"You're stallin' so's they'll reach the yard."

"No I'm not. I told you the truth."

Baxter said no more for a while, but he remained a couple of yards from Dunaway, staring. For Dunaway, the man's appearance inside the barn had been a surprise, although with everything else occupying the attention of the *vaqueros* and their wives, it probably had not been hard for him to slip in from out back.

"How are you going to get back to your horse?" Dunaway asked, then had a sudden thought. "I'll give you what money I have on me." He did not have much. He hadn't had much even before he'd pitched some greenbacks at the feet of Juan-Pedro Althazar in the Mex-town *cantina* yesterday.

Baxter cocked his head at the sound of wheels turning on dry axles. He had made a serious miscalculation in assuming that Dunaway would have kept the money. *He* would have kept it. Worse than the miscalculation was the fact that if he did not get it, the humiliation would be compounded, because within moments now he would have to disarm Dunaway, then back out of the barn and try to get back to his horse, acting like a cornered rat.

For Dunaway, whose understanding of the gunfighter's motives went beyond getting the money back, but nowhere nearly as completely beyond as the situation warranted, it was clear that Baxter could not continue his indecision much longer. They could both hear the mourning party coming up to the north end of the yard.

Dunaway was good with a gun, but no one was good enough to draw, cock and fire when someone was already holding a cocked Colt pointed at him.

Dunaway tried one last time to prevent a disaster with himself as its victim. "Baxter, using me as a hostage might get back the money, but it'll also get you run down and killed. Those men coming into the yard fought a renegade named Seth Wolf, and his outlaw-band, to a standstill yesterday. They killed about half, captured the others, and left Seth Wolf propped against the jailhouse wall dead as a stone. You're not going out of here alive unless you get out right now."

Baxter hadn't been listening until half way through what Dunaway had said, then he stared. "Seth Wolf ...?"

"Yeah. And about eight or nine of his men – half dead, half in the Matanzas jailhouse."

Baxter made his decision. "Walk to the back of the barn. First, drop that sixgun."

Dunaway obeyed by shucking his weapon, then by walking toward the back of the barn. Beyond were the working corrals, about ten or twelve of them all connected by intersecting gates. North of the corrals was open country except for a few trees upon the lip of an erosion gully. Over all of it, bright sunshine shone.

Baxter walked back and told Dunaway to lean out and tell him if there was anyone out there. Dunaway leaned, saw no one and said so. Baxter swung an overhand blow, the barrel of his Colt dropped Dunaway without a sound. Baxter glanced over his shoulder, sprang outside of the barn with his gun swinging, saw no one, and sprinted toward that arroyo in the middle distance.

Out front, Chalo and Onix tied their horses at the rack and Carter Alvarado led his animal inside to be off-saddled. He stopped, stared, and called out.

Chalo, Onix and several other men entered the barn and ran down where Alvarado was bending over the unconscious form in the rear opening.

From northward where the trees grew, movement caught Onix Cepeda's eye. He lifted his head in time to see a rider spur up the far side of the arroyo, break over the top and, still frantically spurring, race northward in a flat-out run.

Onix cried the alarm, pointed, then ran back through to the tie-rack out front, pulled a horse loose, and while the startled animal was whirling, vaulted over its back.

By the time the others got to their horses, Onix was a mile away in furious pursuit. They could see the man another mile onward who had come up out of the arroyo. Without delay all the other men scuffed a dust-streamer to life as they also rode in pursuit.

The *vaqueros* were in their best clothing. None of them had carbines and it was only because of custom that they had even worn handguns to the burial ground.

Baxter had a Winchester which he sought to use in order to discourage his nearest pursuer, a leathery old *vaquero* who was closing up fast, and who was riding with a sixgun balanced backwards in his upheld right hand.

Onix made no move to change course when Baxter fired. Onix had lived a long and colourful life. No one knew how many times he had been at both ends of this kind of chase. Nor would they ever know. But out of all those times Onix Cepeda knew one fact for a certainty; there was no possible way for even a marksman to hit what he aimed at while firing a Winchester carbine off the back of a running horse.

With a pistol a man might do better, but even then what was required was luck more than marksmanship.

Onix did not return the fire. Far back he could hear his companions yelling. He did not look around. Baxter fired three times then faced forward and using the barrel of the carbine, drummed on the rib-cage of his straining mount, and still Onix gained.

The others could not close the distance although they certainly tried, shouting and waving weapons in their excitement. Chalo was screaming grisly promises about what he intended to do when they caught the man they were chasing, but like the others he had no idea it was the same man they had found trussed like a turkey on the floor of the barn last night. All any of them knew was that this man was seen fleeing right after they had found Cab Dunaway lying inertly with blood running down his face.

Onix estimated the distance, urged his horse onward, made a corrected estimate, then stood in his stirrups to minimise the jolting, aimed and fired. He had not tried to hit the man, just the horse. It was a very large target.

The horse seemed to spring into the air in mid-stride and hang there for a second, then he dropped with all four legs folded. The impact hurled Baxter ahead and sideways. He was dazed, but not too dazed to realise his peril. He had lost the Winchester and wasted only a moment trying to find it. But that was a fatal mistake because he did not need the saddlegun anyway, the nearest pursuer was bearing down on him within sixgun range, rawhide-coloured dark skin cracked wide in a death's-head smile.

Baxter struggled to arise. At the same time he lunged frantically for his holster. It was empty. He had lost both weapons. He stood crouched, eyes bulging, as the old *vaquero* came up in a dead run, aimed and fired from a distance of about forty feet. Baxter's hair seemed to rise from the top of his head. He dropped in a threshing heap as Onix Cepeda began to haul in his horse, but not rapidly. He let the animal come back down to a trot, then a walk, and turned to go back where his companions were standing, cooling out the horse on the way.

Twelve:
The Lady

The men argued inside the barn. One of the sweaty *vaqueros* had torn his best white shirt on the saddlehorn as he had swung off near the dead gunfighter, and that did nothing to improve his mood as he watched other men unload the corpse in the runway.

There was some cryptic and uncomplimentary conversation. They had not expected the dead man to be the same man Dunaway had ordered off the place last night, but neither were they surprised. One man was lifting off his saddle when he said, "That ground is very hard, up there." Another rider agreed. "We should have rolled him down a gully."

The man with the torn shirt glowered. "He can't be buried up there, near *el patron* and the others who were decent people."

Chalo Gutierrez flung his saddle on the pole and led the sweaty horse out back to a corral without saying a word, but when he returned and they were fiercely arguing, he finally said, "Before God all the dead are equal. What have the women done with *el jefe*?"

Carter Alvarado was leading his horse away when he answered. "Go find out. As for the gunfighter, Chalo is right. We will make another hole up there."

The man with the torn shirt turned in disgust to address the rangeboss, but Onix Cepeda spoke first, looking directly at the disgusted rider. "The dead are neither good nor bad, companion, only dead."

"He is unfit, Onix."

"No. Only when he was alive."

The disgusted man stamped out back leading his horse. He remained unconvinced, but they had ganged up on him. Further protest would do no good.

Chalo left the barn, but halted only a few feet from the doorway gazing in the direction of the bullet-riddled main-house. He turned and slowly re-entered the barn to address Carter Alvarado. "There is a buggy with a fine chestnut horse ..." He pointed.

Alvarado went to the opening to look, then told Chalo to go ask the women what they had done with Dunaway, and remained as he was, studying the elegant vehicle with the handsome horse over at the main-house tie-rack.

Some short remarks back down in the barn indicated that the men were taking the gunfighter over behind the harness pole to be covered with canvas until he could be hauled northward and buried. Alvarado started walking in the direction of the buggy. He was two-thirds of the distance when Chalo came out of a *jacal* and lumbered forward, softly calling. Alvarado halted to wait. When Chalo caught up he said, "It is *el patron*'s daughter." He paused and they exchanged a stare. They both knew Francisca Stuart, had known her as a child and right up to the time she had married a man who owned a store up in Durham and had gone north to live. She had not been back since. Alvarado scratched, eyed the house, and said, "How is it that she arrives now?"

"Who knows? Manuela said she drove into the yard when they were carrying *el jefe* out of the barn to doctor him, and she told them to take him to the main-house."

Alvarado thought about this too, and stopped scratching. "Did they tell her about her father and all that has happened?"

"Yes ... She already knew."

Carter frowned. "How could that be, it only happened yesterday?"

"She knew, because she told them that she knew."

"Well, I will go see about this."

Chalo had a very strong curiosity. "Do you want me to accompany you, then, companion?"

Carter was gazing in the direction of the house, and shrugged. "No, friend ... Send someone up there to prepare another grave ... *Chihuahua!* What will happen next!" As he said this Alvarado walked away leaving Chalo's curiosity unsatisfied.

The door was still hanging by one hinge when Carter got up there, but it had been propped open.

Inside, daylight shone and someone, probably the women who had laid out James Stuart, had put the overturned furniture back in place but it would require more than that simple gesture to remove the coal-oil slick on the floor, to cover the bullet holes in the walls and over the fireplace, to sandstone bloodstains over in the far doorway where James Stuart had died. Also, the place did not smell pleasant to Carter as he pulled off his hat and went over to the dingy hallway and down it toward the sound of voices.

Cab Dunaway's eyes were sunken and ringed with a bluish look. He was bandaged and lying out full length under several blankets in the very old carved oak bed in which *el patron* had slept for most of his life. Seated on a chair at his bedside was the woman Carter Alvarado remembered very well, except that now she was different, fuller and perhaps even slightly taller, but that could have been because of the way she was dressed. She had very dark eyes, black hair, and a complexion like fresh cream. She had been beautiful even as a child. The last time Carter had seen her she had been six years younger than she was now. That had been the day her new husband had handed her up into a fine top buggy and they had departed after the wedding. Six years had made a difference.

She raised her eyes to the doorway when he appeared, her expression grave. He made a small smile and nodded his head. She said, "Where is he, Carter?" as though they had never been apart. He understood and glanced at Dunaway, whose sunken eyes were also on him. "He is dead, *Señora* ... He is in the barn."

She put aside the bowl of hot beef broth she had been spooning into Dunaway, regarded Carter for a time, then arose and crossed over. He opened his arms and she put her head on his shoulder as she said, "He didn't tell me, Carter. I had no idea until I got a telegram yesterday from the mayor of Matanzas. How could all of this happen?"

She straightened back and Carter looked gravely at her. "It happened, *Señora*," he told her in Spanish. "We buried your father and the others this morning ... Then there was the other one." He glanced in the direction of the bed. "How is he?"

"Injured," she replied in the same language. "But in a week or two he will be recovered ... Who were the others?"

Carter mentioned names and the beautiful woman was silent. Carter eased past and went to the bedside. "Onix shot him, *jefe*, after a hard chase. I didn't think it would happen any more after yesterday."

Dunaway considered the drawn, pale face. There were some good men on the Stuart ranch. Different, but good men. "I didn't think it would happen any more either, *amigo* ... Do you think those cattle we brought back should be pushed up farther from the south range?"

Carter nodded. "Maybe tomorrow." He turned toward Francisca Stuart, eyed her briefly on his way to the door, and from the opening he said, "We will bury the gunman then we will get back to work," and left them alone.

Dunaway watched the handsome woman. It was she he had seen first, after regaining consciousness, but it had been the women from the *jacals* who had washed and bandaged him.

The wound had looked worse than it was. If he had not been wearing his hat it might have been worse, but the old hat absorbed some of the blow. Even so, his scalp had been torn open and he had bled quite a bit before the woman found him. He had no feeling of pain, which was a marvel. He did not know that he had been given laudanum and until it wore off there would be no pain. He simply felt exhausted and weak.

The handsome woman returned to her chair and picked up the bowl of broth without a word. Their eyes met occasionally as she fed him, but she seemed occupied with thoughts which only peripherally included him.

He knew who she was because she had told him, but he had no idea how she had happened to arrive at the ranch until he heard her tell Carter Alvarado about the telegram. Then he remembered the man with the gold teeth and the top buggy which had yellow running gear.

About the gunfighter Dunaway felt nothing one way or the other. Perhaps if Baxter had been brought back alive, he would have felt differently. His only reflection about the Baxter affair was that the man had been a fool, otherwise he would not have risked getting killed for a hundred dollars.

He had noticed the thick gold wedding band on

the beautiful woman's finger. He had also noticed her beauty; even ill and tired to the bone as he was, Dunaway was still a male.

When she had fed him the last of the hot broth and straightened back to put the bowl aside, he said, "*Gracias.* That's about all the Spanish I know."

She studied him. "Will you tell me why you were here?"

He told her, and when she asked about Baxter, he told her about her father sending for Baxter. Then he also said, "Baxter couldn't have done it by himself. No one man could have."

"You did, Mister Dunaway."

"No ma'm. There were nine of us. I was just one of nine."

She continued to study his face. "We owe you a lot. The women told me how you went after those men."

"Lady ... I drank a glass of wine with your father, and we talked." Dunaway considered leaving it at that, but she leaned forward and said, "My father was not a violent man, Mister Dunaway. He lived for his cattle, for this ranch, and for his people."

Dunaway returned her steady dark gaze, and spoke to her from the heart. "Your father ... impressed me like that, and more. He couldn't have done anything with one gunfighter but get himself killed for trying. He needed at least a half-dozen like Baxter. But that kind is no different from Seth Wolf and his kind. Your father ... To me it seemed that he really had no idea what he was up against;

what was happening ... I guess I went after those Texans for him, but there was also a pregnant woman, a little kid, and some others."

She leaned back in silence, and ranged a slow look around the old room with its massively ornate carved furniture. Then she arose saying, "Excuse me," and left him alone.

He slept and did not open his eyes again until the world was very dark and silent. He guessed it was the pit of the night. Someone had been in while he had slept because there was a small bottle of red wine and a glass upon the bedside table.

He had a headache which was dull rather than throbbing. For a while he listened to the hush and had scraps of disconnected memories crowd through his mind. If Baxter had not struck him down he would by now have perhaps been twenty miles away. Lying in this big old bed fully relaxed was pleasant, but Dunaway, who had seldom been ill in his life, had never been able to lie still for long. Even weak and tired as he was, before sleep returned he made up his mind to be on his way in a day or two. The wound was not in a location where it would interfere with riding, and if he rode slowly, there should be no ill effects, and he had no need to ride otherwise because with the working season well advanced, when he got back up north there might not be any work anyway.

The next time he opened his eyes Chalo Gutierrez's squarely-built dark wife was beside the bed, rough hands clasped, gazing down at him. When he looked up she said, "Good afternoon."

He looked around where dazzling sunshine coming through the window filled the room with brilliance and warmth. It was indeed afternoon.

She had an amused look in her eyes and bent to lift the bandage on his head, examine the injury and make a little clucking sound as she re-settled the bandage. "I will change it," she announced. "And this time there must be plenty of grease otherwise it will stick to the cloth. Are you hungry?"

He was, in fact, hungry, and smiled at her. "Like a bear."

"*Bueno*. That is the best sign. Drink some of that wine and I will bring food. Does your head hurt?"

It did not really hurt, but when he moved a little ache came. "No, I'm fine ... Baxter?"

"They buried him this morning. Then they went down for the cattle. They will cut out the injured ones and bring them to the corrals to be doctored." The dark eyes remained upon his face. "There were some men here this morning from Matanzas to talk to you. They were told you could see no one. They wanted to hire you as the Matanzas constable. They were going to offer you a lot of money."

Dunaway looked pained. "They don't have enough money, *Señora*."

Her eyes brightened slightly. "My husband told them that, but they said they would be back in a few days. My husband is a good judge of men, *Señor*."

"Your husband, *Señora*, is a good man – period."

The brightness lingered in her dark eyes, but she shrugged her shoulders without agreeing. Then she said, "The lady will look after you herself," and the dark eyes turned mildly speculative. "Now I will go after your meal."

Dunaway waited until he could no longer hear her footsteps, before pushing aside the blankets and easing up into a sitting position on the side of the bed. Dizziness came like a grey cloud. He waited until it had receded then put both feet to the floor, but the dizziness returned. Today was not the time for him to get dressed and be on his way. He got back under the covers.

When the meal arrived it was a heaping plate of *frijoles* and barbecued meat. There was no coffee, he was supposed to drink the red wine instead. There were corn-ground *tortillas* to eat with instead of a knife and fork, and there was enough for two men.

He was unaccustomed to both *tortillas* and *frijoles*, and could eat the meat with his fingers, but when he finally decided to try the beans he did as he had remembered seeing *vaqueros* do, he tore off small bits of the *tortillas*, made small scoops of the pieces by holding them between his fingers and began eating. The beans were laced with some kind of hot sauce. He ate half of them then reached for the bottle of wine.

Thirteen:
Something To Think About

He heard the riders bringing in the gather and was about to leave the bed to watch from a window when Francisca Stuart arrived. Today, she was attired in light pearl grey. The dress almost looked dusty. As she moved toward the bed she neither smiled nor spoke, but nodded her head and when Dunaway pointed toward the chair she remained standing.

She had appeared concerned for him and she still did, but she had not appeared genuinely friendly. Not even when he knew she felt that what he had done was the result of his feelings for her father.

He mentioned the cattle, which made her liquid dark eyes rise to the window through which the noise was coming. "I remember that sound from early childhood," she told him with no trace of emotion, then finally went to the chair. She asked how he felt, if he liked the food, why he had not finished the bottle of wine, and when during the course of their conversation he told her he felt very well and would leave the next day, she seemed to be suddenly shocked into silence. Eventually she said, "I don't think you should. You feel better, and you look better, but you don't have all your strength back. It will take perhaps another week."

He gazed at her thinking that another week in that big old bed would be more than a man could stand even if he were dying. He told her he was not going any place in particular; just that he wanted to feel a horse under him and see the sun and some blue sky. "Head north, back the way I rode when I came down here. Go up into Colorado north of Raton."

She asked if he had ever been in Durham and when he told her he had passed through Durham on his way south, and in fact it had been someone in Durham who had told him to ride in a direct line and cut off some miles to Matanzas, she gazed at him in a way which made Dunaway think that after asking her question, she had lost interest and had not heard his answer.

After she left he wondered if the fact that he was in her father's bed, or perhaps the fact that he was still on the ranch, and that she really would be glad to see him leave, was what made her seem so detached, at times almost as though while she knew he was there, he shouldn't be.

It made him uncomfortable. It was not by choice that he was there. It had not been by choice that he had arrived on the ranch in the first place.

That evening when Carter and Chalo came in after supper to visit and tell him how it had gone at the corrals, he asked them without a shred of tact if Francisca Stuart had always been a little aloof, or at least a little withdrawn. They exchanged a glance. Chalo became intrigued by the carving on one of the bedposts and Carter Alvarado sat gazing at Dunaway for a long time, then finally said, "She grew up here. There were the women to help after her mother died. She was not very happy for a while after the death of her mother. But that passed; at least she did not seem as sad as at first. No, she was a happy little girl ... Well, her father did not approve of the man she wanted to marry. Afterwards, she never returned to the ranch. Not until yesterday. It was for six years."

"She and her father argued about her marrying this feller?" asked Dunaway.

Carter shrugged. "I didn't hear them argue. But I knew them both. So did Chalo. So did everyone else. When the wedding was over and she drove away, *el patron* was very busy with the cattle and horses. One time after we had worked a very hard day he sat on a log beside me and said, 'Why does anyone work so hard, for nothing?' "

"What did he mean?"

"I don't know, *jefe*. I didn't ask. It was for him to say things but it was not for any of us to ask about them."

Chalo, who obviously had not liked this exchange, moved restlessly in his chair, and finally Carter arose to depart. From the doorway he said, "We will shoe your horse tomorrow."

Dunaway sat propped in bed gazing at the empty

doorway. His horse needed new shoes, but had that been something Carter had offered from the goodness of his heart, or was it something he had been told to do because someone wanted the horse ready to ride when Dunaway got aboard him?

Francisca did not return that day. Chalo's wife fed and shaved Dunaway, her round, dark face expressionless, and where she had often teased him slyly, now she answered his questions and volunteered nothing.

Dunaway had had enough by the third day. After breakfast he got out of bed and crossed the room, sat down until his legs stopped quivering, then arose and repeated it. He was over by the window fully dressed, leaning to look out into a magnificent morning when Francisca appeared in the doorway and stopped stone still looking at him.

He turned. Neither of them smiled. "It's time for me to ride on," he told her candidly. "I'm right obliged for your hospitality, and I'm sorry I had to be such a nuisance and all."

She entered the room slowly. "You were never a nuisance. What we all owe you we could never —"

"Lady, I've heard enough of that kind of talk to last me a lifetime," he told her bluntly. "Nobody owes me anything. I'd like you to answer one question: Did you tell Carter to have my horse shod?"

She had a way of allowing little silences to come between them before she spoke. She did that now. "I was at the corrals and one of the riders pointed out how long the feet of your horse were. I grew up with horses, Mister Dunaway, I know what causes contracted heels. Yes, I asked Carter to have him re-shod."

What she had said about contracted heels was true, and that left him not knowing whether what he suspected was a fact or not. What he had wanted to determine was whether she wanted him off the ranch. What he had got from her reply was an idea of how much she knew about horses.

"You should sit down," she told him.

"Why?"

"Because your face is red."

He said, "Yeah," and went to a chair. They looked at one another for a long time before he spoke again. "I wish I understood you. But it don't matter. Thanks again for all you've done."

"Mister Dunaway, I would like to make you an offer."

His eyes widened.

"The ranch needs a tophand."

He continued to stare at her. "You have Alvarado, and you have the others, Chalo, Onix, Epifanio ..."

She suddenly sat down. "Mister Dunaway, my father lost over a thousand head of livestock. Before that, he lost a few now and then. ... I loved my father very much."

Dunaway watched her beautiful features and read the struggle before she went on speaking.

"When I was a child my grandfather was alive. Things were so different then. He died and my father kept up the customs – but nothing was the same any more. Now my father is dead – what was it you said, something about he couldn't have begun to oppose those renegades by hiring just one gunfighter? Well, that was my father. A kindly, gentle man. Do you know what I am telling you?"

Dunaway thought he knew. "Lady, you have some very loyal men out yonder. They could have got themselves killed down at Matanzas last week, for this ranch."

She considered the hands in her lap. "I know all of that. Their loyalty and bravery are not the problem. They have grown up on the ranch. They reflect my father's beliefs and those of my grandfather. This is what I'm trying to explain to you. Where you come from are things the same as they were seventy-five years ago?"

Seventy-five years earlier, where Dunaway had worked the ranges, there had been no domestic cattle, no towns or ranches or much of anything else, but he did not mention this because he was beginning to understand the drift of her conversation. He arose and returned to the window. From over there, looking back at her, he was about equal parts disturbed by her suggestion, and her beauty.

He said, "Lady; I'm a *gringo*. I don't even speak the language. I'm an outsider, a stranger. If I took the job and stayed here for five or ten years, I'd still be the *gringo*."

She lifted her head and turned toward him. There was a little crease between her eyes as though she were close to smiling. "No. I understand how you feel about being a stranger here. The language is easy to learn, but that's not necessary. Most of them speak English. But what you don't understand is that what you've done for – the ranch; for them; for their people who were murdered ... It is their nature to never forget, either something someone does for them or to them. You haven't been a stranger since you took them after those Texan renegades."

He said, "Naw. Lady, as your tophand I'd be bumping someone else. Maybe Chalo Gutierrez."

"You wouldn't because on this and the other old land-grant ranches, they have never used tophands. Only *mayordomos*, then the *vaqueros*."

He leaned against the window sill gazing at her and slowly wagged his head. He'd been working range cattle all his mature life and understood the way cattle outfits were organised and operated – north of Raton.

She arose. "Whatever they pay up north, I will pay you. Mister Dunaway, this is a large ranch and for two generations my family has been up-grading the livestock."

He had seen enough of the animals to know this was true.

"But it can't be operated as a sort of feudal holding. I loved the old ways too, but they are just no longer possible if a ranch like this is to make money."

He stared at her. "What does that mean? What about those people out yonder?"

"It means simply that from now on Stuart Ranch is going to be operated as a business. The people belong, of course. I've known most of them since I was a child. They are like blood relations to me." She was silent for a while, looking steadily at him, then she said, "What have you seen here that wouldn't be tolerated up north on a big ranch?"

He had seen plenty, but all he said was: "You are a hard person to understand."

"Why? Because I don't want to lose another thousand head of cattle to thieves? Because now that I have to run this ranch, I want to do it in a way so that I won't lose it to bankers some day? That will happen, Mister Dunaway. I've seen it happen dozens of times because *los viejos* would not change and begin operating their ranches as businesses instead of as feudal holdings where all they did was pat children on the head and officiate at the weddings and fandangoes, and race their horses against each other."

Her eyes flashed, her colour was high. He thought she was probably the most beautiful woman he had ever seen. And he also thought she was probably right in what she said. "And if I don't take the job, you will find someone else."

She nodded at him. "I can't do anything else, can I?"

He let go a long, silent sigh and returned to the chair. So this was what had been on her mind since she'd come back; he had known there had been something, but for some reason he could not properly analyse he had not thought it had anything to do with the ranch.

She said, "Well; do you want to think about it

until the morning?"

He slowly smiled up at her. "You might be hard to get along with," he said, arising slowly to face her. She was tall for a woman, perhaps half a foot over five feet. He was about medium height for a man, so he did not have to look down to meet her gaze.

"You could see whether I am or not, Mister Dunaway. I don't think I would be."

"I'd do some thinking," he told her. "All right if I talk to the *vaqueros*?"

He nodded and walked out of the room. For a while, as he continued to stand there looking after her, he had an uneasy feeling that it wasn't the ranch that made her seem so detached or preoccupied. At least it was not altogether the ranch.

"Hell," he muttered to himself, and wandered back to the window to gaze down in the direction of the corrals. Three *vaqueros* were working a green colt up to a snubbing post in the afternoon sunlight. One man was holding a blindfold, another had a saddle balanced upon one hip while the third man was using an extra wrap on the post to pick up slack each time one of the others flipped a pebble at the colt's rump, to make the horse spring forward.

This, at least, was something they seemed to do the same way up in Wyoming, or down in central New Mexico. Dunaway looked around for his hat before leaving to go out there and watch. The damned hat would not fit over his bandage. He flung it irritably aside and strode through the house without it.

It did not occur to him that he might be weak from lying in a bed so long, but by the time he reached the working corrals he was sweating, and it was not that hot a day.

One of the *vaqueros* was a young man; the same young man who had grown up so fast down in Matanzas. He balanced the saddle to one side and came over where Dunaway was leaning to smile and say he was very glad to see Dunaway up and around again.

The man who was snubbing called sharply. He and the other *vaqueros* were fitting the blindfold and the saddle was to go on next.

But they *did* do things differently in New Mexico. The colt was dazed from being choked-down, and when they gave him slack he planted all four feet wide, his body quivering all over, and because he had never been deprived of his sight before, he stood like a stone while they cinched up the saddle. One of the *vaqueros* then stepped up, grabbed an ear, pulled the colt's head down, and as the other man took off the rope and the youngest man was ready to mount, the man holding the ear put his head down and bit, hard.

That same moment the youngest rider swung up, got both feet into the stirrups, made a swift adjustment of the horsehair reins, and because the colt was thinking only about the pain in his ear, he scarcely realised there was a man on his back until the ear-gripping *vaquero* jumped clear.

He threw up his head and did not move. Did not

even turn his head or wring his tail. He was petrified with fear. He was also terrified by his loss of sight.

The young man stroked his lathered neck and spoke gently to him. He rocked a little in the saddle and continued to talk. If this had a calming effect on the colt it was not discernible to Cab Dunaway.

The rider stroked the quivering horse farther up the neck. When he could reach the corner of the blindfold, he gave a quick tug, the blindfold fell, the rider sat back, far back against the five-inch cantle, and there was not a sound from any of the other men.

Dunaway forgot the sweat and the slight trembling weakness in his legs.

The colt rolled its eyes, its lower lip snapped open and closed like a rat-trap. Water dripped from its belly-hair. The man on its back moved a little from side to side. The colt's ears went almost flat back but it still retained that spraddle-legged stance. The *vaquero* brought his legs close to the horse's sides very gently, and simultaneously pulled slowly upon one side of the continuous rope rein. The colt resisted rein-pressure so the rider rolled a spur rowel along his lower ribs.

The colt felt that pain, and in one perfectly coordinated movement got his legs fully under his body, fought to bog his head, bawled like a wounded bear and broke away bucking as hard as he could, but unless he had been able to get his head fully down, he could not buck to his maximum capacity, and this was why the *vaquero* had evened-up the reins and had them held short.

The older men laughed and hooted. Dust flew, the young *vaquero* made a death-head grin, but that was bravado because he was riding for his life.

The colt had not been saddled nor ridden before. He had been handled and broken to lead, but this was his first trip out with someone on his back. It was rarely the first ride that lost a rider, if he was much of a rider, it was the second ride, after the colt had had all night to think things over. On the second ride, the youthful *vaquero* wouldn't smile.

The *vaquero* got the colt's head shoved into a corner. The battle ended over there. The *vaquero* came down from the saddle with the swiftness and grace of a cat. He talked to the lathered colt with the bloodshot eyes, and gently tugged it around then led it back to the snubbing post. As he passed Dunaway, the youth swaggered just a little. The older men laughed.

Dunaway was smiling when he returned. Francisca Stuart was standing five feet away. It startled him because he'd been concentrating so hard on the colt and rider he'd heard no one coming up.

She said, "When he was a baby I used to change his diapers."

Dunaway glanced over where the buckaroo was off-saddling while Carter Alvarado held the colt snubbed. He looked back at her grinning. There was probably nothing anyone could have said at this moment which would have been more incongruous; the *vaquero* was standing hipshot-loose, making it appear that what he had just done was all in a day's work, but his eyes were bright with pride. If he had heard what she had said …

She had something else to say, and she said it while watching the men in the dusty corral. "I want you to ride out with me in the morning."

He waited but she did not elaborate, so he nodded. "All right."

She lingered a short while then turned back in the direction of the main house and as Dunaway watched her go, he had a little trouble with conflicting emotions.

Chalo came over and slapped Dunaway on the back, settled himself along the corral stringers and wagged his head. "Today he is the chief rooster. Tomorrow the horse will be different." He turned from watching the buckaroo carry his outfit toward the barn. "You look good. Manuela said it was a bad gash."

Dunaway eyed Gutierrez who, despite his very dark, villainous appearance, had proved to be a man of courage, resourcefulness and humour. "I'd like to talk to you, Onix and Carter."

Chalo spread his hands. "Now?"

"Yeah."

"I will get them. Over at the shoeing shed?"

Dunaway nodded. That would be a good place. It was private and apart from the other buildings. Chalo turned in the direction of the barn and Dunaway rolled and lit a smoke, his first in several days, and it made him slightly light-headed so he dropped it and ground it underfoot.

Then he strolled over to the shoeing shed where

morning heat had not reached, and stood looking at the old forge, the anvil on a huge oak stump, the sooty ceiling and the forge and fitting tools arrayed in leather loops. It was a very old building in which many men had left a lot of sweat.

Fourteen:
A Springtime Day

The following morning as Dunaway held the stirrup for Francisca Stuart he was thoughtful and unsmiling. If she noticed she said nothing about it, but as they left the yard she waved to several of the men who were harnessing a team to go after firewood, and smiled as they waved back. She seemed to be different from what she had been up until today, at least Dunaway got that impression as they rode northward with the sun on its upward sweep – and a number of people back in the yard watching them go.

She looked well on a horse. He had never doubted but that she was a good rider, and she was. When they were loping westerly from the little cemetery hill she glanced over there, and afterwards said nothing until they had covered a couple of miles.

There were cattle on this side of the west range, and there was a distinctive division he had not seen before, between her land to the south, and that immense, flat and wind-scourged country to the north over which he had ridden several weeks ago. It was almost as though Nature, or whatever was responsible for such things, had drawn a straight, narrow line, and had decreed that everything north of the line would be arid, thin-soiled, semi-desert, while everything south of it would have trees, water and grass.

He was intrigued by this when she said, "Carter came to see me last evening."

His attention was brought back. But he said nothing. He had rather suspected one of them would talk to her after the palaver at the shoeing shed.

"He wants you to stay."

Dunaway looked at her profile. It was as perfect as the profile he had once seen on a cameo. She turned. "They liked your frankness when you talked to them."

He smiled at her. "It was just that I didn't like the idea of moving in on someone else's territory. Carter is the foreman, Chalo and Onix are his tophands. I know, you told me and they did too, that on Mex cow outfits they don't have tophands. But bosses get to rely upon some riders more than others. It amounts to the same thing, whether you folks have a name for it or not."

She returned his level gaze. "That's what they like about you, Mister Dunaway, you consider the feelings of other people."

That made him uncomfortable and he shifted slightly in the saddle and turned to look at some nearby cattle. They had good quality bred into them.

She probably sensed his discomfort because she suddenly turned brisk. "We will start marking tomorrow. The men will bring in wood for the branding fires today. It will take about two weeks."

He turned back toward her. All right; he had the job, and he did not object to that. He even rather liked the idea. But there remained the *haciendada* herself. He could do the work, and he could learn the different things they did down here which he was not accustomed to. But how long would it last if he and his employer did not understand each other?

He finally put it into words. "Lady, doing the job don't worry me. How long you'll want me around does worry me." He saw her eyes widen and pushed on before she could speak. "I don't know what it is, but there's something about me you don't like. Don't deny it. I didn't come down in the last rain. I sensed it the day I opened my eyes and saw you sitting next to the bed, and since then I've noticed it more ... I don't want to work for anyone under circumstances like that."

He was poised to say more, but restrained himself. He had put it bluntly because he knew of no other way to get it out into the open.

She faced forward and rode a few yards, then shifted direction slightly aiming for a bosque of trees in a broad, wide, grassy swale. "We will talk," she said, almost formally, and led the way to that shaddy, secluded place.

She dismounted and tied her horse, then stood gazing southward with her back to him until he had tethered his animal and was looking at her back while tugging off his roping gloves.

Without facing around she spoke quietly and matter-of-factly. "This had nothing to do with you taking the job." She allowed one of those little interludes of silence to intervene, then spoke again. "I married a man six years ago. He did not like my father and my father did not like him." She turned toward him slowly. "I can shorten it – but it was six years happening. My husband had some friends. They did not come to Durham." She looked steadily at Dunaway. "They worked together; he knew which stages of his own company, and other companies, were carrying mail and bullion ..."

Dunaway let his breath out silently and fished around for his makings. He kept his eyes lowered as he rolled the cigarette. He knew what she was going to say.

"For six years they robbed stages. Not always. My husband was not a fool. He let some bullion shipments reach the banks. His friends then robbed the banks."

Dunaway lit the cigarette and looked at her. It was almost like seeing a different person. Her expression was unrelentingly bitter.

"Last year two U.S. marshals came to see me at our house in Durham ... They had been building a case against my husband and his friends for almost a year." She sighed and stepped back into tree shade before continuing. "They showed me a lot of written pages, and some stage company invoices. They were kindly men. When they had finished talking to me they told me to sit down ... They had known a particular robbery was to take place, and they were lying in ambush."

Dunaway dropped the half-smoked quirley and stamped on it.

"... They put his wallet on a table in the parlour, and the gold watch I had given him as a wedding present with both our initials inside a heart engraved on the case ... they put that beside the wallet."

Dunaway waited.

"He was dead." She turned. "It was the first I knew about any of it, Mister Dunaway ... but ... the marriage had not been a happy one ... My father had been right. I could not admit that, so I did not come back home ... Men," she said almost fiercely, and moved closer into the shade with the bitterness of that last word like a stone wall between them.

He watched her for a long time, then also moved into the shade. So it had not been him she had disliked, it had been men. All men.

Then she said, "But I want you to take the job. I have to make the ranch successful." She turned, very erect and pale.

Dunaway gazed at her from fifteen feet away. She had not mentioned her husband's name, but yesterday the *vaqueros* had told him: It had been James Carlin. And they had told him something else; there had been a child, a baby girl. It had died before reaching two years of age. That was all they had mentioned, but as he stood gazing at her now, he thought that if they had known the rest of her story, they would have told him that too.

He removed his hat and ran bent fingers through his curly brown hair. She had told him she would not be hard to work for, but if she hated men, how could she not be hard to work for? His desire for the job atrophied but he did not know how to tell her, so he said, "I'm sorry, for all of it. I liked your father. Like you said, he didn't belong in a world where renegades can take over a country and kill people and steal cattle unopposed."

Her eyes were misting and that bothered Dunaway, so he spoke sharply to her. "Do you think for one damned moment that you're the only one who's made a mistake? If we had the time I'd tell you about some bad ones I've also made. At least you had something to go back to. Lady, wounds heal but they leave scars. I know how that is. I also know that thinking about bad things for a year or two ruins people." He saw the tears welling up and moved over, opened his arms and closed them around her. "Let 'em flow. But you're making an even worse mistake to think all men are like that. They aren't."

She leaned fully against him without making a sound, but he felt the silent sobbing tear at her. He had nothing more to say so he held her as though she were a child until she was able to place both palms against his chest and push, then he released her, fished around for his blue bandana handkerchief and pushed it into her hand.

Because he did not know what else to do he started talking about the range, the cattle, the good weather which usually came in springtime to make rich feed, and when he looked at her again she was tearless and white, and drooping. He said, "Sit down."

She sat with her back to a tree avoiding his eyes and she held out the soggy bandana to him.

He squatted and rolled another cigarette, which he lit, then held it out to frown at it. "They don't taste good any more," he said more to himself, in surprise, than to her.

She spoke again still without looking at him. "They aren't good for you anyway."

He killed the quirley. "My mother told me that when I was twelve years old."

"... What was she like, Mister Dunaway?"

"A little like you. Very pretty ... and she knew more sorrow in her lifetime than I think you'll ever know. She buried four babies before my father died."

"Is she alive now?"

"No."

Silence settled between them broken only by one of the horses shifting position then making a snuffling sound. He settled his body against the warm ground with his head propped upon one arm looking at her. She saw him doing this and seemed uncomfortable so he said, "How old are you?"

It startled her. Her eyes flashed at him, and he smiled at the unspoken rebuke. "It don't matter anyway. What I was thinking was that you've probably got fifty, maybe sixty, years to go down the trail, as opposed to maybe twenty-three or four years you've already travelled. Look out there at that grass and sunshine, smell the springtime in the air." He stopped speaking but did not stop looking at her.

She held out her hand for the bandana and he handed it back to her. A moment later she balled it up and kept it in her hand as she quietly said, "What bothers me most is that I never came back."

Dunaway suddenly remembered something Carter Alvarado had said to him; it was about her father saying something about there being no purpose in a man working hard. He understood what her father had meant. Her father had known about the child which had died, and he had known his daughter would not return.

He had nothing to say. In fact he suddenly felt drained dry.

She made an unsteady sigh and did as he had said, she looked out beyond their fragrant and shady place at the miles of golden, rolling grassland, and because it had always had a soothing effect upon her, even as a child when she'd had no particular need for soothing, she spoke in a dull-soft tone of voice.

"I'm tired, Mister Dunaway."

He pulled a blade of grass and chewed on it.

"I feel tired and old."

"That's today," he told her. "You can't feel that way for fifty years ... Sure beautiful country isn't it? Tell me something, how do those curlicue Mex brands show up so well on cattle without blotching where the welds are?"

"Because there are no welds, Mister Dunaway. They bend the iron and hammer it and form it."

He nodded.

She looked down at him. "You aren't at all like the men I met in Durham, Mister Dunaway."

He tossed the grass stalk away. "Sure I am. I cuss and get mad, and don't get my hair cut when I should. And the first time you land on me for something I do around the corrals you don't like, I'm going to jump right back with all four feet." He laughed and sat up sweeping off grass. Without changing his smile he also said, "You want to give me a chance at this job?"

"Yes."

"You're plumb sure about that?"

"Yes."

"All right. Now do me a favour. Give yourself a chance too ... Come on, I'd like to ride over more of the land." He spoke and held out a hand to her. She gripped his palm and as he pulled her to her feet, he said, "Do I call you boss, or – what?"

They were very close so she quickly stepped back before turning toward the horses. She did not answer until she was astride kneeing the horse up beside him as they left the trees and rode out into the sunlight. "Boss ... That doesn't sound right, does it? Is that what they call women who own ranches up north?"

He had never worked on a ranch owned by a woman so he did not know. "They don't call 'em by their first names. I know that much. But what else they call them ... What's wrong with boss?"

"There is no Spanish word for that, exactly."

"Well, what do I call you?"

She pondered. "*Señora*?"

"All right. But my first name is Cabot. They call me Cab, not Mister Dunaway – *Señora*."

They loped for two miles, until she hauled down to a steady walk as she pointed to a stand of uneven trees in the middle distance and told him that was the all-year creek which cut diagonally across seven miles of Stuart range. She also showed him an old adobe shack, roofless now with its mud walls dissolving under winter rains. Her grandfather had lived in that place as a very young man while he had been developing the ranch.

They rode to the creek, drank, watered the horses, and as they mounted again he sat gazing at her. She turned back in the direction they had been riding and said, "We must build back up to four thousand cows."

He accepted that. "And salt," he said. When she looked around he said, "Make salt logs and put them along the creek. That way you can nearly always make a count without riding yourself bowlegged. Cattle need salt."

She continued to watch him. "And – what else?"

He was riding on a loose rein with both gloved hands resting on the saddlehorn, squinting into the sun-bright distance.

"Build up over maybe five or six years by holding back the best-framed heifers out of cows that have had at least three calves."

She got squared-up in the saddle during one of

those little silent interludes, and finally said, "Thank you."

He looked around in surprise, ready to speak, but understanding came before he made a sound. He smiled and, remembering something Chalo's wife had said when he had thanked her, he tried it out on his companion. "*Por nada.*"

Her eyes brightened toward him. "I told you it was an easy language to learn."

They had rooftops in sight before she spoke to him again. "Are you hungry?"

He was. Neither of them had eaten since before leaving the yard that morning. "Yes'm. Are you?"

"Maybe a little ... Not very much, though. This has been a good day for me."

He watched tiny figures far ahead unloading wood from a wagon near the corrals behind the barn.

"I feel better, Mister Dunaway."

"Cab."

"I feel – like I've gotten over an illness."

He leaned to lightly rest a gloved hand atop her hand on the saddlehorn, and grinned. "You have, God willing, but it don't happen in just one day. It's something a person's got to work at." He leaned back with his hand going back atop his own saddlehorn. "That's quite a pile of wood they brought in."

"I told you, it will take about two weeks to get all the marking done. That means a lot of branding fires." She glanced sideways at him. "You'll learn a lot of Spanish during those two weeks."

They both understood what she meant by that. He would learn a lot of swear words. He did not tell her he already knew enough of those words. "Maybe the next time we head out over the range you could help me pick up the language."

She nodded. "I will."

That was as near as either of them came to saying they needed each other's company.

They came down toward the back of the barn where a great stack of dry wood had been pitched at random. There was no one around. He led both horses into the barn to be unsaddled and she followed, and as he flung up a stirrup-leather to tug loose a latigo she said, "I – I think I'd better go over to the house."

He nodded, busy unsaddling. She lingered a moment more, then walked away without another word. He dropped the stirrup-leather, lifted off the saddle, and stood like that watching her cross the yard. In the place of what had been between them before, there was now something different. He flung the saddle over the pole and leaned on it, thinking.

If it hadn't been for that bitter wind a couple of weeks ago, none of this would have happened. He went over to unsaddle the other horse.

